STEELE

A CHRISTIAN ROMANTIC SUSPENSE

LAURA SCOTT

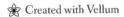 Created with Vellum

CHAPTER ONE

Harper Crane huddled in her winter coat as she hurried along the snowy sidewalk. She absolutely hated parking in downtown Milwaukee, especially in January, but it couldn't be helped. Her role as a legal assistant at Gibson and Roberts Law Offices meant showing up at the high-rise building four days a week. Her boss, Trent Gibson, let her work from home every Friday, unless he had depositions scheduled in one of the conference rooms.

Shivering, she increased her pace. The surface parking lot she used charged ten bucks a day. The structures were more than twice that amount, so she ducked her head against the wind and pushed forward. The office building was only five blocks away.

She was so busy watching her feet to make sure she didn't slip and fall that she didn't pay attention to the vehicle coming up beside her. Even when it idled in the road, she didn't think much about it. When the back passenger door opened and a man emerged, her instincts finally kicked in.

Danger!

A hard hand grabbed her arm. No! She tried to tug out of his grip, her stupid office flats slipping on the icy pavement.

She opened her mouth to scream, but he ruthlessly clamped his other hand over her mouth and began dragging her toward the car.

The silent scream lodged in her throat as she struggled against his grip. This couldn't be happening. She couldn't allow him to get her into the car!

"Police! Get your hands where I can see them!"

The shout came from her left. The assailant instantly let her go, shoving her backward, then diving into the back seat of the car. The driver hit the gas and careened away from the curb, tires squealing and horns blaring as he rounded the corner and disappeared. A cop chased after the vehicle, but then stopped and turned to jog back toward her.

Harper landed hard on her backside, her arms instinctively curling around her pregnant belly. She couldn't breathe, couldn't do anything but stare up in horror as the uniformed police officers rushed to her side.

"Ms. Crane? Are you okay?" The fact that the dark-haired cop knew her name wasn't reassuring. She stared up into his blue eyes, trying to comprehend what had transpired.

"We need to get her up," the other officer said.

"Okay, easy now." The cop with dark hair and blue eyes slid his arm behind her shoulders. With the help of both men, she managed to get back on her feet. Her body was sore, especially her tailbone, but she relaxed when she felt her baby moving. Should she go to the hospital to be checked out? She wasn't sure that was necessary but didn't want to take any chances with her baby's life.

"Can you tell us what happened?" Her gaze landed on

the dark-haired cop's name tag. His last name was Delaney. The other officer's name tag read Greer.

"I—have no idea." She pushed the words through her tight throat. "Out of nowhere, this guy came out of the car and tried to kidnap me."

The two cops exchanged a glance. Delaney nodded. "Yes, ma'am, we know that much. Did you recognize the man who grabbed you? Did he say anything?"

"Why would I recognize him?" None of this seemed real, although clearly it was. If not for these two men showing up in the nick of time . . . she swallowed hard. "No, he didn't look familiar." She thought back to those tense moments when she'd belatedly realized what the guy's intent was. "He didn't say anything. Just grabbed me, clapped his hand over my mouth, and dragged me toward the car . . ." She broke off, shivering.

"Okay, that's fine. We had to ask." Officer Delaney spoke in a soothing voice. "Brock, did you get his license plate number?"

"Yeah. Sent it to dispatch to issue a BOLO on the vehicle," Officer Greer said.

"We'd like you to come down to the precinct to look at some mug shots." Officer Delaney smiled reassuringly. "I'm sure your boss won't mind. We can call the law office from the squad, explain that you need some time off."

Her boss at the law office? Time off? The hairs on the back of her neck rose in alarm. These cops knew her name. They knew where she worked. They probably knew more about her personal life than her boss did.

Realization sank deep. They hadn't just gotten there so quickly by chance. She narrowed her gaze at Officer Delaney. "You were following me? Watching me and following me? Why?"

Delaney held her gaze for a long moment. "It's best if you come with us. We can discuss this in more detail at the precinct."

Somehow, she sensed it would be better for them—not her—to go along with the plan. Yet someone had tried to kidnap her. This—she didn't understand any of this. Her shoulders slumped, and she slowly shook her head. "This is about Jake, isn't it?"

"You tell us." Officer Greer arched his brow.

She scowled. She didn't like him. Either of them. They'd been watching her. Waiting for something bad to happen. And it had!

With an abrupt move, she twisted away from Officer Delaney, shouldered her purse strap, and walked away. She wasn't going anywhere with them.

"Ms. Crane," Delaney called her name as he quickly caught up with her. "You can't just pretend this didn't happen. Don't you realize you're in danger?"

"Why?" She spun to face him. He was so close that her belly bumped into him. He hastily stepped back as if burned. "I don't understand. My ex-husband is dead! He can't testify. There's no reason for anyone to come after me. To try to kidnap me!"

"Clearly, someone associated with your ex-husband wants something from you." His placating tone grated on her nerves. "Please, come with us to the precinct. We really need to talk."

Her baby kicked again, and she put a hand to her abdomen beneath her coat to soothe her unborn child. She was just over seven months pregnant. Stress wasn't good for either of them.

"Fine." She turned to face him. "But you better be prepared to share what you know too. I want answers,

Officer Delaney, especially if me and my baby are truly in danger."

The cop's gaze dropped momentarily to her abdomen before bouncing back up to meet hers. "I understand."

Did he? She wasn't convinced. Yet she didn't have much of a choice but to go along with them. Not if she wanted to understand exactly what was going on.

She reluctantly allowed Delaney to escort her back to where his partner Greer waited, hoping and praying she wouldn't regret this.

STEELE COULDN'T BELIEVE Jacob Feldman's pregnant ex-wife had almost been snatched right under their noses. The near miss would earn them a scowl from their bosses, Lieutenant Joe Kingsley and Captain Rhy Finnegan. Both guys were fair and decent men, but they also held high standards.

He would take full responsibility for the incident. He and Brock had been watching her from a distance. He hadn't anticipated those guys would try to grab her during daylight hours, early in the morning no less.

It was concerning to know Harper was pregnant and in danger. She was right; none of this was her fault.

He was certain the actions of her ex-husband had dragged her into this mess. What Harper didn't know was that Feldman wasn't killed in prison the way she'd been told.

No, the weasel had decided to testify against his coconspirators, so his death had been faked. Easy enough to do after he'd gotten beat up in prison bad enough to require a trip to the hospital. He was currently being held in a safe house down in Chicago. The truth would be revealed when they got closer to trial.

Someone else obviously knew Feldman was still alive. Maybe they'd even decided to abduct Harper as leverage against Feldman hoping to get the guy to change his mind about testifying against the big boss, Tommy Grotto.

Either that or someone believed Harper knew more about Feldman's illegal activities than she'd let on.

Considering the way Harper had filed for divorce exactly twenty-four hours *before* Jacob Feldman was arrested, he felt certain she had discovered key information related to his illegal activities.

A theory that seemed to have been the motive behind the abduction attempt.

Glancing at her in the rearview mirror, Steele took note of the way she stared out the window without saying a word.

"Did you want us to call your boss?" he asked, breaking the silence.

Her jaw tightened, but she shook her head and pulled her phone from her purse. "I'll do it."

He and Brock exchanged a glance as she made the call, explaining to her boss, Attorney Trent Gibson, about how she'd been attacked and was being taken to the police station for questioning.

"I promise I'm fine, and so is the baby," she said. "I don't know how long this will take, though."

Another silence as she listened to whatever her boss was saying.

"Okay, thanks, Trent. I appreciate that. I'll let you know." She lowered the phone, then asked, "Does my boss know about you two following me?"

"No, we've never met him." He held her gaze in the

rearview mirror. "We only know that he's your boss."

"Yeah, sure." Her tone indicated she didn't believe him.

Brock shrugged and looked away. Steele could tell that his fellow teammate didn't trust Harper Crane any more than she trusted them.

He pulled into the parking lot of the third district police station, then threw the gearshift into park. He pushed out from behind the wheel, then quickly jumped out to open the back passenger door for Harper, knowing she couldn't get out of the caged area on her own.

"Be careful," he warmed, taking her elbow. "It's slippery."

She gave a curt nod and allowed him to escort her inside. Brock followed behind, covering her back without being asked.

Whoever had tried to grab Harper could easily try again. A fact he wasn't sure she really appreciated.

"This way." He steered her through the maze of cubicles to one of the interview rooms. "Have a seat."

She did, then crossed her arms over her chest. "How long is this going to take?"

He stifled a sigh, dropping into a chair across from her. "Ms. Crane, we need to understand how much you knew about your husband's business dealings."

"Ex-husband." She held his gaze for a long moment, then added, "I didn't know anything. I had no idea he was about to be arrested."

He didn't believe it. "You're saying it was just a coincidence that he was arrested twenty-four hours after you filed for divorce?"

A flicker of uncertainty darkened her green eyes, but then she nodded. "Yes. I—he'd changed. He became withdrawn, terse, angry, and verbally abusive." She dropped her hands to her pregnant belly. "He'd morphed into a completely different person from the man I'd married two years ago."

Steele swallowed a sigh. He'd hoped she'd be more forthcoming after nearly being kidnapped off the street. "Those guys tried to grab you for a reason, Ms. Crane. Have you considered what might have happened if we hadn't been there?"

"Yes." Her voice was a whisper. She closed her eyes for a moment, then lifted her gaze to his. She was stunning with her long blond hair and bright-green eyes. And for a moment, he had to wonder if the abduction was for another, more sinister reason. Sex traffickers didn't normally target pregnant women, but it was possible they hadn't known about her condition. If he hadn't been watching her move around inside her apartment, he might not have noticed either. Her winter coat was big enough to cover her rounded belly.

"I neglected to thank you and Officer Greer for saving me," she said, as if having come to the realization that arguing with them wasn't going to work in her favor. She frowned. "Although I have to admit it's more than a little disconcerting to realize you've been watching me, following my movements."

He wasn't going to apologize for keeping an eye on her. They'd run out of leads and had decided to keep tabs on Feldman's ex-wife. He was secretly glad they had. "You know this attempt to grab you must be related to your ex-husband. We need you to tell us everything you know to find the men responsible." He paused, then added, "Before they try again."

"Again?" She paled. "You think they will?"

"Ma'am, you need to come clean right now." Brock's

curt tone betrayed his impatience. "Tell us who grabbed you and why."

"I don't know!" Harper's voice held anguish as she slapped her hands on the metal table. "If I did, I'd tell you! Don't you think I'd do whatever necessary to protect my baby?"

Steele frowned at Brock, silently warning him to back off.

"Yes, I know you would protect your baby in any way possible," he hastened to reassure her. "But, Ms. Crane, we need you to think back. There may be something your husband said that may help us now."

"Ex-husband!" she shouted. Then her face crumpled. "This isn't my fault. I didn't do anything illegal."

"No, you didn't." He reached across the table to take her hand. "I'm sorry you're having to deal with this, but it's going to be difficult to protect you if we don't know who is behind this attempted kidnapping."

She pulled away, swiped at her face, then met his gaze. "I gave the names of my ex-husband's friends to the police when he was arrested. I barely saw Jake for those two weeks before I moved out. I—he caught me leaving with the last box and forced me to sleep with him." Her voice hiccuped, and his heart squeezed at hearing what she'd suffered. "Then he got a call and left the house, saying something about how he'd be there right away. I took it as a sign from God and got out of there as quickly as possible."

"And you don't know who called him? Or what the call was about?" he gently pressed.

"No. I was pretty upset, as you can imagine." She blinked tears from her eyes and swiped at her face again. "I thought the call might be from Starkey. Ellis Starkey is one of his closest friends. But I can't say for sure."

They knew about Ellis Starkey who had seemingly disappeared off the face of the earth, either hiding or dead, and had been hoping for more. "You didn't know about the guns he was buying and selling?"

"No." She held his gaze. "I hate guns, and Jake knew that. He would never have told me he was buying and selling them." She put a hand on her abdomen again. "If I had known, I would have left him much earlier."

She was probably thinking that if she had done that, she wouldn't be pregnant now. He wondered how she felt about that, then decided it was none of his business.

Brock rose to his feet and headed for the door. "I need air," he muttered.

Steele understood his buddy's anger and frustration. They were all running low on sleep since the most recent raid on a warehouse in Ravenswood, one coordinated by the ATF with backup from their tactical team that had ended in a major gunfight where too many of the bad guys had managed to escape. Their teammate Flynn had been nicked by a bullet, but thankfully, they had killed three men. Getting one or two alive would have been better, but that hadn't happened.

The bad news was that Ellis Starkey and Tommy Grotto, along with a third guy by the name of Waylon Brooks, were still in the wind.

And those were only the guys they knew about. He and the rest of the tactical team suspected there were others too.

Having illegal guns flooding the streets had led to dozens of shooting incidents, with more on the horizon. As if being a member of the tactical team wasn't dangerous enough. They were being called on to participate in more takedowns and tactical situations than ever before.

"Ms. Crane," he began.

"Please call me Harper," she interrupted. "Ma'am makes me feel old. And I'm not accustomed to people calling me by my maiden name." She shook her head. "I was such a fool. I thought Jake was perfect for me, that we'd be married for decades the way my parents were. But I couldn't have been more wrong."

"I'm sorry, Harper." Using her given name made it difficult to remain professional. "But keep in mind Jake created an illusion. You couldn't have known the truth he kept hidden for so long."

"I won't make that mistake again," she murmured. Then sighed. "I wish there was more I could tell you. Truly. But I swear I don't know anything."

He believed her, yet that meant there was likely only one reason they'd attempted to kidnap her. And that was to force Jake into not testifying. Someone within the Grotto organization must realize he wasn't dead.

He had to keep that thought to himself, though, as he wasn't cleared to share any details of their investigation with her.

"Okay, there's one last thing we need from you." He rose to his feet. "I'm going to gather several mug shots for you to look at. I need you to tell me if any of the men look familiar."

"I can do that." She hesitated, then said, "Thank you, Officer Delany. I appreciate your kindness."

"You may as well call me Steele," he said, turning toward the door. "I'll be back in a few minutes."

As he stepped outside the interview room, he found Joe Kingsley and Brock Greer standing there.

"You sure she's not hiding anything?" Joe asked.

He could tell Brock had given Joe an earful. "Anything is possible, but I find it difficult to believe she'd hold back from us knowing her baby is at risk. She doesn't have any love for her ex-husband either."

Joe nodded thoughtfully. "Yeah, I heard enough to agree with you. Brock, as you know, still has his doubts. Pull together those mug shots and see if she can identify anyone."

"Sure thing." He knew Brock had trust issues from recent events in his personal life, so Steele let it go. For his part, he couldn't help but feel bad about her situation. Maybe because he was still grieving the loss of his girl-friend, Monique.

He found Raelyn putting the mug shots together for him on the computer. It was easier and faster than using paper or lineups.

"I heard the perps got away," she said without looking at him. "I have Gabe Melrose, our tech guy, searching street camera footage for the vehicle."

"Thanks." He appreciated Rae's chipping in to help. Despite being a talented cop, she was always willing to offer her assistance in any way.

Jina, on the other hand, balked at doing what she called scut work. Unless, of course, Joe or Rhy personally assigned tasks to her. He didn't mind working with the handful of female cops on their team, but Jina had a chip on her shoulder the size of Everest.

He grabbed the closest laptop and booted it up. Within five minutes, Rae had sent him the six-packs she'd put together. He brought each of the three groupings up on the screen, then minimized two of them.

Carrying the laptop to the interview room, he placed it in front of Harper. She looked surprised, then leaned forward with interest to study the first group of six men.

She took her time, studying each face for a long moment

before moving on. But at the end, she sat back. "I'm sorry. None of these guys looks familiar."

"That's okay, let's try the next one." He hadn't expected her to identify Tommy Grotto; the guy was a chameleon, blending into his surroundings. He brought up the next group of six faces.

"That's Ellis Starkey." She pointed at the face in the middle of the bottom row. "I didn't realize he'd been arrested."

"He hasn't; we just happened to get a good picture of him." He minimized that screen and brought up the last six pictures.

She studied them, then shook her head again. "Nope. Never saw any of these guys before."

He shouldn't be surprised that she hadn't been able to identify Waylon Brooks. He glanced up at the one-way glass and gave a small shrug.

Disappointed that they hadn't learned much from this interview, he closed the laptop. "Okay, thanks for your help."

"Does this mean I can go back to work?" She looked surprised and a bit apprehensive.

He hesitated. Joe hadn't mentioned getting approval for a safe house for her. "Yes. I'll drive you back to the law office. However, you really shouldn't go anywhere alone." Team members would continue keeping an eye on her, but that wasn't foolproof. If they'd been a few yards farther back, they may not have been able to rescue her in time.

"Okay." She stood and reached for her coat. He found himself holding it for her so she could slip her arms into the sleeves. "Thanks."

"You're welcome." He cleared his throat, reminding himself that she was a victim of a crime, not a potential date.

And pregnant to boot. He wasn't interested in going down the relationship path again. He gave himself a mental shake as he opened the door for her, glad to see both Joe and Brock weren't still hanging around.

"This way." He still had the keys to the squad, so he didn't bother to find Brock. It didn't sit well with him to drop Harper off at the law offices, but he escorted her outside anyway.

She didn't say anything until he pulled up to the skyscraper housing the prestigious law offices of Gibson and Roberts. Ironically, their specialty was criminal defense. They made their money defending people like her ex-husband. "Off—er—Steele, will I be safe going home tonight?"

"Do you have friends or family you can stay with?"

"Not really. My parents passed away last year." She grimaced and reached for her door handle. "Never mind. I'm sure I'll be fine."

"Hold on." He slipped out from behind the wheel, raking his gaze over the area as he went around the back to her side. He opened her door for her. "I'll walk you inside."

As she emerged from the squad, the sound of gunfire reverberated around them.

"Get in! Keep your head down!" He shoved her back down inside the squad and used his radio to call for backup. When another bullet shattered the windshield, he hunkered down behind the vehicle, trying to pinpoint the location of the shooter.

The answer to her question was a big fat no. Harper Crane was far from safe. And he still wasn't sure why she'd been targeted.

CHAPTER TWO

What was going on? Harper huddled down in the front seat of the squad, trying to make herself as small as possible. Why were men who'd worked for her ex-husband trying to kidnap her?

To kill her?

Her belly made it impossible for her to get her head down very far, barely hidden behind the dashboard, and she silently prayed for God to protect her.

Please, Lord Jesus, please? Keep us safe in Your care!

The prayer didn't calm her nerves as the wail of sirens split the air. Her body trembled from fear or the cold. Why was this happening?

"Harper? Are you okay?"

Steele's voice pierced her thoughts. Cautiously, she lifted her head just enough to see him standing near her passenger-side window.

She belatedly realized the windshield had been struck by the gunfire, the glass shattering inward. Nothing hurt, but she ran her hands up and down her arms anyway to be sure. Thankfully, she didn't find any blood.

"I—don't know." Fear had gripped her brain, making it difficult to think clearly.

"Come on, we're getting you out of here."

She didn't move. "Where?"

"Your vehicle. Come with me, hurry." Steele gripped her arm and tugged her from the squad, leaving her little choice in the matter. He surprised her by clamping his arm around her shoulders and half covering her body with his.

The parking lot was five blocks away, but somehow, the distance didn't seem as long as it had earlier today.

Was that really only ninety minutes ago?

Her stupid shoes slipped on the icy ground, but Steele was holding her so tightly against him that she didn't fall. His arm was like a vice around her, giving her the sense that he'd pick her up and carry her if she couldn't keep up.

"Keys?" His voice was a low rumble near her ear.

"Uh, in my purse." How she'd managed to hang on to her purse through all of this was a mystery. She managed to get the bag up so she could grab the key fob. She didn't have a fancy car, just a plain, ordinary blue Chevy sedan.

He took the fob and quickly unlocked the car. Then he helped her slide into the passenger seat. She didn't protest, even though it was her car. Her fingers were still trembling so much she doubted she'd be able to drive.

Steele pulled out of the parking lot, heading in the opposite direction of the law offices. Glancing at her, he reached over to crank the heat on high.

As if that would help her to stop shaking.

"Wh-where are we g-going?"

"Far from here" was his grim response. He glanced at her briefly before turning his attention to the road. "That was too close."

You think? She bit back the snarky comment because it

wasn't fair to take her anger out on him. Not when he'd done everything possible to protect her and her baby.

She pressed her hands to her abdomen, willing herself to stop trembling. She wasn't hurt. Her baby was fine.

That was more than enough for now.

Steele's radio crackled. "Steele? Where are you?" She thought she recognized Officer Greer's voice.

"I'm taking Har—er—Ms. Crane someplace safe."

"Where?" Greer demanded.

"I don't know yet. See if Joe or Rhy will get us a safe house."

"Fine, but stay in touch, we're spreading out to search the area for the shooter." The radio fell silent.

The idea of a safe house was both reassuring and horrifying. It was nice that Steele cared enough to keep her safe, but how long would she have to stay there? She forced herself to think logically. "You believe someone wants me dead because I know something about Jake's illegal arms dealing." She made it a statement, not a question.

"Yes." He shot her a quick glance. "Unless you have another reason for bad guys to come after you?"

"No." She thought briefly about some of the criminals her boss represented. Men and women who had been accused of terrible crimes. There was one guy recently who made her skin crawl, but there would be no reason for Neil Otterson to come after her. Not when her boss was doing his best to keep him out of prison.

She didn't like the exposure to criminals. Trent always reminded her that every citizen deserved a fair trial, and that could only happen if there were good lawyers like him to help make sure the cops and DAs got it right.

Trent Gibson liked to compare himself to the fictional character of Mickey Haller from Michael Connelly's books, although his record for getting his clients off wasn't nearly as impressive. Real life wasn't the same as fiction.

"What about one of your boss's clients?" Steele's question seemed to pick up on her thoughts. "If this isn't about Jake, is there a reason one of Gibson's clients would come after you?"

"He is defending several clients, one big one in particular, but I'm not a lawyer, so it doesn't make sense for him to come after me." She drew in a deep, calming breath. "Trent is married and has two kids. If any of his clients were upset with him, they would target his family. Not a lowly office assistant."

He nodded thoughtfully as he navigated the streets of Milwaukee. He'd taken so many twists and turns she soon had no idea where they were. Some area of the city she didn't normally enter, based on the boarded-up and run-down homes lining the streets.

It didn't take long, though, for them to enter a nicer neighborhood. She realized they must have been heading east, as they'd arrived at White Gull Bay, a nicer suburb not far from Lake Michigan. When Steele pulled up to a dark-gray ranch home, she frowned. "Who lives here?"

"Me." He parked in the driveway, then pushed out of the car. "Wait for a moment."

She did as he suggested, the recent shooting still fresh in her mind. If Steele hadn't reacted so quickly, the outcome could have been bad.

Very bad.

Swallowing hard, she unbuckled her seat belt as he opened the door for her. She noticed Steele scanned the area as he ushered her to the front door. A moment later, they were inside.

The warm interior was nice, decorated for comfort

rather than looks. There was a plush sofa in an L shape and several watercolor prints on the walls. Her knees felt weak, so she made her way to the sofa and sat down. "How long have you lived here?"

"Four years." He shrugged out of his MPD jacket and crossed over to join her. "Are you warm enough?"

At some point during the drive, she'd stopped trembling. "Yes." She unzipped her coat as the warmth soaked into her skin. "How long are we going to be here?"

He eyed her curiously. "As long as it takes."

She blinked in confusion. "What does that mean?"

"We're staying here until the upper brass finds a safe house for you." He didn't sit but rose and paced the area. "That shooter was waiting for us, as if knowing I'd drop you off at the law office sooner or later."

His words drew her up short. "You mean, he was watching and waiting the same way you and Officer Greer watched and followed me."

"Yeah. I guess you could say that." He scowled. "There must be something you know, Harper. Some reason your ex-husband's cohorts in crime have come after you."

"I don't know anything!" She didn't hide her sharp tone. "Why don't you believe me?"

"We're missing something," he muttered to himself.

"Look, even if Jake had told me something about his business dealings, what's the point of coming after me now? He's dead; he can't testify."

Steele stopped and stared at her for a long moment. Then he sighed and jammed his fingers through his dark hair. "Jake Feldman isn't dead. He's being held in a safe house out of town."

"What?" She instinctively wrapped her arms around

her belly as his confession sank deep. Her ex-husband was still alive.

And he'd done or said something that had placed her and her unborn child directly in the line of fire.

———

HARPER LOOKED shell-shocked by the news. He hid a wince, knowing Joe and Rhy wouldn't be happy that he'd told Harper the truth about her ex-husband. Yet he couldn't keep lying to her. Besides, the more she knew, the more she'd cooperate.

He hoped.

"Your ex has agreed to testify against Tommy Grotto," he said. "After Jake was beaten up in jail, he decided it was in his best interest to give us what we needed to put Grotto away for the rest of his life."

"In exchange for what?" she asked, her voice hoarse.

"Witness protection." He crossed over to drop beside her. "I'm sorry, Harper. But it's obvious Grotto or his allies know your ex-husband is still alive. And I think they're trying to get to you to force Feldman's hand."

"Force his hand how?" She tucked a strand of her long blond hair behind her ear.

He had to admire her grit. Harper Crane hadn't fallen apart as he'd feared. "If Grotto can get his hands on you, he can threaten to kill you if Feldman doesn't back down."

Before he'd even finished speaking, she was shaking her head. "No way. That's ridiculous. Jake couldn't care less about me. He'd never sacrifice himself to save me."

Her blunt assessment startled him. "But you're carrying his baby."

"Yeah. The baby he hadn't wanted." She turned to look

at him with a solemn expression. "Trust me on this. Jake wouldn't care if I was killed. And the baby too. That's not what's going on here."

Then what was? He wasn't sure how to respond since that was the only theory that had made any sense.

His radio squawked. Rising to his feet, he moved away from Harper to respond. "Go ahead, Brock."

"No sign of the shooter but we found a 9x19 mm Parabellum shell casing. Possibly from a SIG Sauer P226, just like those that we found in that warehouse in Ravenswood."

The same type of handguns Jake Feldman had been dealing, although that ammo could be used in other weapons too. "What are the chances of picking up prints?"

"Not very likely," Brock said. "The casing has been sent to the lab, but I wouldn't hold your breath."

He knew his teammate was right. The shooter had likely worn gloves, especially in the cold winter temps. "Anything else?"

"We're pulling a mangled slug out of the squad now," Brock said. "Not sure it will be much good. Boss wants to know where you are."

"Safe." He didn't want to admit he'd brought Harper home. Brock, Joe, and Rhy would have a field day with that. It hadn't been that long ago that he'd lectured Joe on getting too emotionally involved with Elly, a woman he'd been protecting. He could easily imagine Joe turning his words back against him. "What's the status on a safe house?"

"Joe and Rhy are looking into it." Thankfully, Brock didn't press for more information. "Let me know where I should meet you."

"I will. Later." He quickly ended the radio transmission. He'd bought them a little time, hopefully long enough for Joe and Rhy to come through with the safe house.

It bothered him to know an innocent pregnant woman was in danger. Monique had died in a car crash from a drunk driver heading the wrong way on the interstate. His girlfriend had been in the wrong place at the wrong time. Was that what happened to Harper?

Maybe not since her ex-husband is a known criminal. And criminals didn't care about the sanctity of life. He'd seen a lot of bad stuff working as part of the tactical team over the past three years and as a street cop for four years before that.

Sure, there were plenty of good people in the world. It just so happened that he was exposed to those who were the exact opposite.

Whatever. This was what he'd signed up for. After his older sister, Amelia, had been killed by her stalker ex-boyfriend, Steele had made it his mission to protect the innocent.

And you couldn't get any more innocent than Harper Crane and her baby.

Maybe keeping them safe would help him heal some of his grief over losing Monique and Amelia. Two women he hadn't been able to protect.

Shaking off those troubled thoughts, he turned to face Harper. "Would you like coffee? Or breakfast?"

"I don't suppose you have herbal tea?"

He hated crushing her hopeful expression. "No, sorry." He didn't know a single person who drank herbal tea, then belatedly realized she was avoiding caffeine because of her pregnancy. "I have decaf, though."

She nodded. "Okay, that works. Thanks."

"I'll be right back." He gratefully ducked into the kitchen. He needed to get these overprotective instincts under control. Yes, she was pregnant and therefore more vulnerable than other witnesses. But he couldn't afford to be distracted by her condition.

As he made a pot of decaf coffee, he silently acknowledged the smartest thing would be to hand Harper over to someone else. Any cop could be stationed with her at the safe house. He and the rest of the tactical team were better off being out on the street, trying to find Grotto or his goons.

Yeah, that's exactly what he'd do. Once they had the safe house arranged, he'd drop Harper off and move on with the investigation.

Satisfied, he filled a mug for her, then called out, "Do you want milk and sugar?"

"Milk, please," she responded. "I'm avoiding sugar these days."

He added milk and carried the coffee into the living room. She was sitting with her feet up. It was disconcerting at how easily she made herself at home in his space. "Here you go."

"Thanks." She cradled the mug in her hands as if needing the warmth. "I hope you don't mind. My feet hurt in these stupid shoes."

He arched a brow. "Why do you wear them?"

She flushed. "Because I'm supposed to dress in business attire. Trent Gibson and his partner both wear suits. Being pregnant has made my feet swell, so the shoes don't fit as well as they used to. But I have a pair of slippers beneath the desk in my office. I can usually get away with wearing the slippers for a big chunk of my day."

Her phone rang, startling them both. She pulled it from her purse, then grimaced. "Speaking of which, this is Trent now. I promised I'd be in to work."

"Let me talk to him." He held out his hand for the phone.

She shook her head, answering it herself. "Hi, Trent, I'm sorry, but it doesn't look like I'll be able to make it in today after all."

He watched her closely, but she didn't give any hint as to what her boss was saying.

"Yes, I was targeted by gunfire," she said, avoiding his gaze. "I'm sorry that I brought danger to the office."

That made him mad. He reached over and plucked the phone from her fingers. "Attorney Gibson? This is Officer Delaney. I'm holding Ms. Crane in protective custody. I'm sure you can understand our concern for her well-being and that of her unborn child."

"Yes, of course," Trent said hastily. "But having so many cops outside the office building isn't good for business."

Why, because you defend criminals? He managed not to say the words. "I'm sure you can agree that an innocent woman and her baby deserve to be safe regardless of the inconvenience."

"Yes, yes, of course. I—uh, just tell Harper, I mean, Ms. Crane that I'll put her out on sick leave. She should take as much time as she needs."

"I will. Thanks for your cooperation." Steele ended the call before he could say something he'd regret. Well, he wouldn't regret it, but Harper might. "Your boss is putting you out on sick leave."

"That will give me less time off after the baby is born." She nibbled her lower lip between her teeth. "I only get six weeks of paid medical leave. I was hoping to extend my time off with personal days."

It struck him that as a soon-to-be single mother, she probably wouldn't have the support she'd need. She'd be taking care of an infant all alone.

And why did he care? Harper's maternity leave wasn't any of his concern.

"It's more important that you and the baby are safe." He tossed the phone between them and rose to his feet. What he needed was distance.

And for Joe and Rhy to get that safe house arranged ASAP.

He returned to the kitchen to fill another cup of coffee. Not that he usually bothered drinking decaf. What was the point? But it was as good an excuse as any to stay away from her.

Yeah, he shouldn't have brought her to his place. Chalk it up to temporary insanity. That, and maybe a soft spot for a woman in danger.

Harper wasn't his sister, Amelia. Yet the situations were similar. If he'd been older, more in tune as to what Amelia had been going through, he may have been able to save her.

But he hadn't. Too busy playing football in high school to pay attention to what Amelia was doing at college.

Sipping his decaf coffee, he tried not to think about how his sister had fought for her life. How her ex-boyfriend had repeatedly punched and kicked her until she'd died.

How no one had heard Amelia's screams.

Enough. He gave himself a mental shake. This whole situation was messing with his head. After losing Monique, he'd locked his emotions in a deep freeze.

This was not a good time for them to thaw out.

"Excuse me, Steele?" Harper hovered in the open space between his living room and kitchen. "May I use your bathroom?"

"Of course." He set his mug aside and headed for the hallway, gesturing with one hand. "First door on your left."

"Thank you." She rested her hand on her belly as she brushed past him.

He glanced at his watch for what seemed like the tenth time in ten minutes. What was taking so long to secure a safe house?

Pulling out his phone, he shot off a text to Joe Kingsley. *Any word on the safe house?*

Three little dots appeared as Joe drafted a message back. *Not yet. Where are you?*

He hesitated, then answered his new lieutenant the same way he had Brock. *Safe.*

Joe replied, *???*

He sighed. Obviously, Joe didn't appreciate his vague answer either. It didn't really matter. They wouldn't be hanging out at his house for long.

Shoving his phone back into his pocket, he returned to the kitchen for his decaf coffee. A glimpse of a brown SUV coming down the street caught his attention.

It was an odd color for a car. One that wasn't highly popular compared to the black, dark blue, dark green, gray, silver, and white models out there. And one that didn't belong to any of his neighbors, as he'd made a point of familiarizing himself with the names and vehicles of those who lived around him.

With a frown, he crossed the living room to look out the window. The brown SUV moved past, then turned left at the next block. He turned away, telling himself to relax.

There was no reason to be on edge. He'd made sure they weren't followed, and the shooter would have no idea where he lived. And the car used by Harper's kidnappers had been black, not brown.

Harper returned to the living area. "Thanks. The baby likes to kick my bladder."

"Ah, sure." He hoped he didn't sound as idiotic as he felt. Babies were not anywhere in his field of expertise. Like Jina, he was a sharpshooter. And he sometimes helped Brock handle hostage negotiations, although Brock was far better at talking people off the ledge than he was. The guy had a calm, soothing voice. Which was kinda funny since his teammate also had serious trust issues. "I checked with Joe Kingsley, our lieutenant. They hope to have the safe house ready soon."

"Okay." She smiled as she sank back onto the sofa. He belatedly noticed she'd kicked her shoes off again. "I'm sure you're anxious to get rid of me."

He wasn't, and wasn't that a kick in the pants? Yeah, he needed his head examined. He forced himself to take a step back, doing his best to sound impartial. "Our only goal is to make sure you're safe."

"I still can't believe Jake is alive." She shook her head. "He must have been hurt pretty bad to have agreed to testify against the guy he worked for."

"He's fine now," he assured her.

She grimaced. "I know I'm supposed to forgive those who trespass against me, but that is far easier said than done."

Considering how the guy had treated her, he completely understood where she was coming from. Yet he sensed she cared about acting the way God would want her to. He'd watched Joe praying with Elly, his fiancée, the same way Rhy did. It was something he and the rest of the team noticed but didn't talk about.

There were times it was easy to believe in God, like when they hadn't lost anyone during the recent warehouse incident.

But there were other times, like when Kyle had been

murdered by a crazed gunman or Monique being killed by a drunk driver, that made it difficult to understand the mere concept of faith.

Movement outside the window caught his eye again. His gaze narrowed as he saw the same brown SUV pass by.

Not a coincidence.

"Put your shoes and coat on," he said curtly as he grabbed his own jacket. "Hurry."

"What's wrong?" To her credit, Harper did as she was told, slipping her feet into the flat dress shoes and reaching for her coat and purse.

"We need to get out of here." The words had barely left his mouth when the passenger window of the car lowered, revealing a gloved hand holding a gun.

The passenger fired several rounds in quick succession, aiming directly at Harper's blue sedan.

"This way. Hurry!" He tugged her through the house to the back door. The problem was that his backyard was surrounded by white fencing. Not chain link that could be seen through, but solid white boards mounted side by side. The previous owner had dogs, and he wished he'd gotten the dog he'd planned on too.

"Where are we going?" Harper's voice was tight with fear. "Is there a way through the fence?"

"No, we're going over it." He led her to the southeast corner of the lot. There was a slight hill there, making it slightly easier to get up and over the fence.

"I can't!" Harper stumbled as he tugged her through the yard. "It's too high!"

"I'll help you." Upon reaching the corner, he turned and made a stirrup with his hands. "Step here. I'll get you over."

"What if I fall?" Her blue eyes were wide with fear and doubt. "The baby . . ."

"Hurry." There wasn't time to debate the merits of the plan. They needed to get away from here.

She stepped into his hand, then gasped when he levered her up to the top of the fence. She gripped the edge and managed to swing one leg over the top, then the other. It wasn't a picket fence, thankfully, but still difficult to do while being pregnant. She hung there for a minute, then let go, falling to the ground.

He didn't hesitate to vault over the fence too. He quickly raked a gaze over her. "Are you hurt?"

Looking dazed, she shook her head.

"Good. Follow me." He took her hand and headed through his neighbor's yard, using his radio to call for backup as they ran.

CHAPTER THREE

Harper had never in her entire life climbed over a fence and had trouble believing she'd done it now, especially while seven months and one week pregnant. Her breath heaved in and out of her lungs as she struggled to keep pace with Steele's long strides. He led her through one backyard and another, her feet freezing in the stupid shoes. As she slipped and stumbled for what seemed like the tenth time, staying upright only because of Steele's strong hand on hers, she silently vowed to never wear them again. She didn't care what Trent Gibson said about office attire, she was showing up in warm running shoes from now on.

If she survived long enough to return to work.

When Steele stopped at the corner of a house, she leaned gratefully against the brick, gulping deep breaths of badly needed oxygen.

"You're doing great," he whispered, his gaze keenly sweeping the area. "Brock will be here soon."

Brock Greer didn't like her, yet she knew Steele's partner wouldn't let his feelings prevent him from keeping her safe. Still, it bugged her that he'd taken an instant dislike to her. She was a nice person. Didn't hurt anyone. Sure, she'd made a mistake marrying Jake, but no one was perfect.

"Ready?" Steele's question penetrated her thoughts.

"For what?" She thought they'd stay there until Brock arrived.

"We need to keep moving." Steele flashed what was likely supposed to be a reassuring smile as he gently squeezed her hand. "Let's go."

Realizing he'd only stopped for her sake, she pushed away from the brick wall. "Okay."

Steele led the way, leaving the yard to reach the street. He turned north, moving past a few houses before once again darting through someone's private property. Considering it was daytime, she found it hard to believe no one noticed them trespassing.

Or maybe they had been spotted, and one of the neighbors had called the police. That wouldn't be the worst thing since Steele was still dressed in his full uniform.

Yeah, that was likely why no one had stopped them.

It didn't take long for her to become short of breath again. Steele slowed his pace, casting a sideways glance at her. "One more block, okay?"

Did she have a choice? She nodded, saving her breath. True to his word, he led her through another yard to the next street. As if on cue, a black SUV turned the corner, coming toward them. Her heart squeezed, fearing these were the bad guys, but she needn't have worried.

Steele raised his hand and paused, waiting for the vehicle to get closer. Then he opened the rear passenger door. "Get in."

Pathetically grateful to get off her aching feet, she did. Steele shut the door, then jogged around to climb in beside Brock.

"What happened?" Brock asked as he drove away.

"At least two men, maybe more, peppered Harper's car with bullets." Steele shook his head. "I don't know if that was merely a warning or if they were planning to head inside my place to find her. I didn't stick around long enough to find out. We left through the back door, climbed the fence, then called you."

"Climbed the fence?" Brock's gaze met hers briefly in the rearview mirror. Was it her imagination or had there been a hint of admiration there? She told herself it didn't matter what Brock thought. Or Steele, for that matter.

"She did great." Steele turned in his seat to face her. "Are you sure you're okay? No issues with your pregnancy?"

"As far as I can tell, I'm fine." She wasn't exactly an expert in the having a baby department. This was her first and likely only pregnancy. There was no way on earth she planned on getting married again. She wasn't even sure how she'd manage to raise this child, but she would do everything in her power to keep her baby safe.

"You need to let us know if anything changes." Steele pinned her with an intense gaze. "We can get you checked out at the hospital if needed."

"Trust me, I will." She hadn't planned or anticipated this pregnancy, and the circumstances were less than ideal. Still, she wanted this baby more than anything, even knowing the child would carry Jake's blood in his or her veins.

This baby was a blessing, a reason to celebrate in her otherwise bleak life. She only hoped that being off work wouldn't risk her job. Raising a child alone would be difficult enough, but not being employed would make it ten times worse. Especially since she'd learned her parents had been in debt when they died. She had nothing to fall back on, other than hard work and determination.

She'd been thankful Trent Gibson hadn't terminated her after her ex-husband's arrest. Maybe her boss had spared her because she'd already filed for divorce. And because he made a living representing criminals like Jake.

"There's a glitch on the safe house," Brock said, interrupting her thoughts. "I'm taking you to a secondary location."

"What caused the change?" Steele frowned. "Clearly Harper's life is in danger."

"Technically, we don't know that the shooter wants her dead." Brock didn't seem to notice how Steele glared at him. "But the truth is, she isn't a material witness."

"What does that mean?" she demanded. "My life and that of my baby don't matter?"

"Of course, you both matter. But we can't use the city's funds to pay for a safe house for you." Steele's tone was grim. Then he addressed Brock. "What's the plan?"

"I've arranged for a rental; it's also in Ravenswood." Brock glanced at him. "Don't blame Joe or Rhy, they did their best. They're always supportive of us. It was Michaels who put a kibosh on the safe house."

"Yeah, I figured," Steele said with a sigh.

She didn't know who Rhy and Joe were personally, but it was clear both men were well liked and respected. It was humbling to know that Steele was doing his best to protect her.

"I booked the place under my name," Brock continued. "But it's concerning that Harper's vehicle was found at your home."

Steele scowled and shook his head. "My fault. I should

have checked to make sure there wasn't a GPS tracker on it. Either that or they tracked her phone."

She felt her pockets, checked her purse, and sighed. "I left my phone on your sofa."

"That's probably a good thing." Brock met her gaze in the rearview again. "Harper, you're absolutely sure you don't know who is behind this?"

She bit back a sarcastic response. "I promise that if I did, I'd tell you. I have no love or respect for my ex-husband." A thought occurred to her. "Maybe Jake hired someone to hurt or kill me?"

"You told her?" Brock demanded.

"Yeah, I think she deserves to know what she's up against," Steele responded. "Whoever is behind this isn't going to give up. Not if they took a chance by coming to a cop's house to grab her."

Brock let out an exasperated sigh. "I hope that doesn't come back to bite you in the butt."

"How could it?" Steele asked. "She's in danger because of her ex-husband. Either—as she pointed out—from him personally or from someone who thinks that taking her will force him into not testifying."

"Okay, okay," Brock muttered. "I see your point."

"Good. Because she's the victim here, bro. Not the perp," Steele shot back.

"Maybe, but we need answers." Brock turned at the next stoplight. "Sooner than later would be nice."

"If I had them, I'd give them to you." She was tired of defending herself. She wasn't a criminal and didn't condone her ex-husband's behavior. Not in a million years would she keep a secret that would place her and her baby in danger.

Swallowing hard, she relaxed against the seat and rubbed a soothing hand over her belly. The baby was kicking again, the movement reassuring. Her feet were still killing her, but all the running and fence climbing to escape danger hadn't caused any permanent damage.

Yet.

A shiver that had nothing to do with the January temperature rippled through her. If these guys kept coming after her, they might cause her to have a miscarriage. Or deliver a very premature baby. Seven months and one week was far enough along for a baby to survive, but only with the expert care provided within a neonatal ICU.

Bands of panic tightened around her chest. No, she couldn't allow that to happen. Drawing in slow deep breaths, she struggled to remain calm. Three months ago, she'd joined the church located just two blocks from her apartment building. She'd found solace and hope there, the members welcoming her with open arms. Like a sponge, she absorbed everything she'd heard about God, their Lord Jesus, and having faith.

She firmly believed God would protect her and her child.

IT WASN'T easy to shrug off his rookie mistake of not checking Harper's car for a tracking device or having her dump her phone sooner. A stupid oversight that had nearly gotten them both killed.

The bad guys hadn't shown up on the street outside her law office by accident. No, they'd known her routine, had watched her maybe longer than the police had.

But why attempt to kidnap her? That was the part Steele didn't understand. If Harper was right about her ex-husband not caring about her, then using her as leverage to prevent him from testifying wouldn't work.

Unless the guys who'd tried to take her didn't know that. After all, she was pregnant with her ex-husband's child.

When his phone rang, he winced, knowing it was likely Joe or Rhy. Seeing Joe's name on the screen, he quickly answered. "What's up, Lieutenant?" Up until a week ago, Joe had been one of them. Now their teammate was technically their boss.

"What were you thinking taking Ms. Crane to your house?" Joe Kingsley demanded. "Have you lost your mind?"

"I was waiting for a safe house." He kept his tone reasonable. "Where else would I take her?"

"Anywhere else," Joe snapped. Then he sighed. "Look, Steele, I appreciate you were in a predicament, but I need to you to remain focused."

"Like you did when Elly Finnegan was in danger?" The comment shot from his mouth before he could stop himself. He winced. "Never mind. I shouldn't have said that. Please know I'm laser focused on finding these guys. I should have expected them to be tracking her car or phone, more likely her car since they shot it up. Did the officers who responded to the scene get anything useful? Shell casings? Bullet fragments?"

"Yes, they found casings and slugs embedded in Ms. Crane's car," Joe admitted. Thankfully, he let the comment about Elly, his fiancée, slide. "The casings appear to be the same as we found outside the shooting at your squad. The lab will let us know for sure."

"Okay." The slugs and shell casings would only come into play if they recovered a weapon for a comparison. "The car I saw was a brown SUV, maybe a Ford Bronco or a Nissan. I don't know how many auto companies make brown SUVs, as it's not a common color. Something to check on."

"I'll run a DMV record of brown SUVs registered in the state of Wisconsin," Joe said. "But that doesn't mean it's not a rental, or even from out of state, like Detroit or Chicago."

According to the AFT, both cities had ties to the Grotto gunrunning operation. "I know. I wish I had a license plate number, but I don't." He thought back to the incident outside his house. "I didn't get a close look at the weapon in his hand either, but it was similar to a SIG Sauer."

"Glocks use the same sort of ammo as the SIG Sauer," Joe reminded him.

"The weapon I saw wasn't a Glock." It wasn't much of a clue, but it was all he had.

"Okay, we'll lean toward the SIG, then." Joe was silent for a moment. "Steele, I know I didn't listen to your warnings the way I should have when it came to protecting Elly. But don't follow in my footsteps. Things could have ended very differently for us."

He glanced at Brock, who kept his eyes trained on the road. "I hear you loud and clear, Lieutenant."

"Stop the 'lieutenant' baloney and call me Joe. The way you always did." With that, Kingsley ended the call.

"What was that about Elly?" Harper asked.

"Nothing." He shouldn't have said anything.

"You accused Joe of crossing the line to protect Elly," she pressed.

"That situation was different, as Elly Finnegan is Rhy's youngest sister." He turned to glance back at her. "Rhy's the captain of our tactical team."

"Oh, I see." Her gaze narrowed. "Special treatment for one of your own."

"Not exactly," Brock said. "We all wanted Joe to step back from the case. It's not smart to mix personal feelings with danger. Tends to cloud a man's judgment."

Steele turned away. "Brock is right. This is very different."

"Yes, I know. I was the one who married a criminal." Her statement didn't hold any bitterness, but it made him feel bad anyway.

"We will both protect you with our lives, Harper," Steele said. "Without hesitation."

"Truth," Brock agreed. Then he let out a surprising chuckle. "Cannot believe you tossed that in Joe's face."

"Didn't mean to, it slipped out." Steele changed the subject. "Tell me about this rental."

"It's a small house in a suburban neighborhood," Brock said. "I got it cheap since it's offseason."

"I'll reimburse you," Steele said. "This is my fault, not yours."

"It's fine." Brock seemed to have softened his attitude toward Harper. "I don't like the way they found your home."

He didn't much like it either. Yet he owned a piece of that. Which reminded him of something he neglected to ask. Pulling out his phone, he called Joe back. "Hey, did anyone find a GPS tracker on Harper's car?"

"Yes, there was one tucked under the front end," Joe admitted. "The tech guys are checking it out now, but it appears to be a basic model that's easy enough to buy over the internet."

It galled him that he'd missed it. "Okay, thanks." He

tucked his phone away. "We need to check out Harper's place. There's likely someone keeping an eye on it."

"I thought you and Brock were keeping an eye on it," she said.

They had been. She lived in a second-floor apartment in Greenland. It was a small brown apartment complex with only eight residences. "We never saw anyone staked out nearby. But that doesn't mean they haven't sent someone there to wait for you."

"I don't get all this." Her low tone sounded frustrated. "There's no reason to target me. Absolutely none. I don't know anything, and despite the timing, I wasn't involved in Jake's arrest."

He empathized with her plight, but clearly someone thought she was important. Why? He wasn't sure. Before he could say anything more, though, Brock exited the highway and turned into a quiet neighborhood.

Minutes later, his teammate pulled into the driveway of a small white house with a one-car detached garage. "This is it," Brock announced.

"It's nice," Harper said with admiration.

There was no reason to feel sorry for her having to raise her baby in an apartment. Plenty of people rented, especially now that real estate prices had skyrocketed to ridiculous levels. Taking Joe's words to heart, he thrust his sympathy aside. All that mattered was keeping her safe. Once they'd arrested those responsible, he'd walk away from Harper Crane, moving on to his next case.

End of story.

He pushed out of the vehicle, going around to help Harper. He caught her wince as she stepped out. "You're hurt?"

"Just my feet." She managed a wan smile. "These shoes

were not meant for fleeing through backyards. I'd much rather have a pair of comfy running shoes."

"I'll see what we can do," he said. Brock raised his brow, but Steele simply shrugged. "We need her to be able to run if necessary."

"Fine, I'll get whatever she needs," Brock reluctantly agreed. "Along with a replacement phone."

Steele held out his arm for Harper, not wanting her to fall on the icy pavement. Despite his assuring her that they could take her to the hospital to be checked out, he'd rather not be put in that position.

That baby of hers needed to stay right where it belonged.

He escorted her inside, then stepped back as she looked around. "This is great." She looked as if someone had handed her a diamond ring, rather than put her up in a safe house. "Although it's a little chilly."

He crossed to the thermostat and cranked it up several degrees. "Have a seat, Harper. Make a list of what you need from the store."

She sank into one of the kitchen chairs. When she kicked off her shoes, he frowned when he saw her bloody toes.

Dropping to his haunches, he inspected her feet. "You have blisters."

"I know." She frowned and shrugged. "I told you these shoes weren't meant for running through yards and climbing fences. I work in a law office; they expect me to dress nice."

"Okay, what size shoes?" Brock asked. "And I assume you'd like some basic toiletries too?"

"Yes, please, including prenatal vitamins." She offered her shoe size, then added, "I wouldn't mind a sweatshirt, too, if it's not too much trouble. These work pants are fine, but the thin top isn't very warm."

"Don't you need specific maternity clothes?" Steele tried to avoid staring at her belly. Personally, he thought she looked cute in her maternity outfit but managed to hold his tongue.

"An extra-large sweatshirt will work just as well." She smiled. "Thanks."

"Get some bandages and antibiotic ointment too," Steele told Brock. "And you should probably grab groceries. At least enough food to last twenty-four hours."

"Sounds good. I'll be back soon." Brock turned and headed back outside. The moment the door closed behind him, the interior of the house seemed to shrink around them. Being here alone with Harper didn't feel any different from when he'd taken her to his house.

He turned away, double-checking the lock on the door for something to do.

"Excuse me," Harper murmured, rising to her feet. He shouldn't have been surprised when she padded to the bathroom.

He sank into the closest chair and rested his head in his hands. Okay, he seriously needed to get a grip. Harper needed his protection, nothing more.

There was no reason to hover over her like some expectant husband or father. Her personal life was none of his business. Any normal person would be extra careful when it came to protecting a pregnant woman.

He couldn't afford to make the mistake of caring for her more than he would any woman in danger. If he'd been smart, he'd have offered to run errands, leaving Brock with her.

Rising to his feet, he went from window to window to

check their surroundings. He didn't see how the gunmen could have tracked them here, but he wouldn't make the mistake of taking their situation lightly. These men were not random guns for hire.

Not that it took a lot of brain power to place a tracking device on her sedan. His thoughts went back to Tommy Grotto, the head honcho behind the gunrunning scheme. At least, according to Feldman.

He wondered if Joe had reached out to their Alcohol, Tobacco, and Firearm contacts, Bryon Perkins and his partner, Steve Banner.

Pulling out his phone to call them for himself, he hesitated. He didn't know Perkins or Banner very well, as the backup request had gone from Perkins's boss to Rhy, who'd agreed to the plan. Their tactical team had helped back up the ATF raid on the warehouse. The one that had turned into a full-blown shoot-out at the O.K. Corral.

This wasn't the first time their team had worked with the ATF, so there was no reason to suspect anything underhanded. Especially since the ATF had also been involved with placing Feldman in a safe house in exchange for testifying against Grotto.

He called Joe, who answered quickly. "What's wrong?"

"Nothing. I was curious if you mentioned the attempted abduction of Feldman's ex-wife to ATF Agents Perkins or Banner?"

"Not yet, why?" Joe asked.

He breathed easier at the news. No way could either ATF agent be involved in the attempts against Harper. "I was just curious."

There was a long pause before Joe asked, "You think the ATF is involved?"

"Not really, but you know how the feds are about not

sharing information. I guess I'm glad you and Rhy decided to keep this latest development a secret."

"Well, it won't be a secret for long," Joe said. "Rhy has a meeting with Perkins and Banner this afternoon."

It made sense that Rhy would be looking for more intel on Feldman and the rest of the gunrunning crew. "Do you think ATF will try to take over the case?"

"Is that a roundabout way of asking if ATF will want to hold Ms. Crane in protective custody?" Joe asked bluntly.

Yep. That was exactly what he'd been thinking. When he didn't immediately respond, Joe sighed loudly in his ear.

"I don't know what Rhy's planning," Joe finally said. "He doesn't brief me on everything."

"Understood. Will you let us know if Perkins or Banner have any new leads?" He turned from the window to see Harper padding back to the kitchen. The blood had been cleaned from her toes, but even from here he could see the reddened and weeping blisters. "The abduction and shooting attempts must be related to Feldman."

"I will. Anything else?" Joe asked.

"No, but thanks for the update. Later." He ended the call, slightly annoyed Joe had read him like a book.

"Did they arrest someone?" The hopeful expression in Harper's green eyes made him wish he had better news.

"Not yet." He resumed the seat across from her. "You said you didn't know your ex-husband's friend Ellis Starkey very well. When was the last time you saw him?"

She frowned. "Maybe a week or two before I left Jake. He made a habit out of dropping by the house unannounced. Or maybe Jake knew he was stopping by but neglected to tell me. I don't know."

"So that was roughly seven months ago?"

"Something like that." She rested her hands on her

belly. "I didn't pay any attention to their conversations. I figured they were talking about business. Legitimate business," she stressed. "I didn't know their company, F & S Enterprises, was a front for gunrunning."

"I believe you," he quickly assured her.

"I assume you checked their warehouses," she said.

"Yeah." He didn't say anything more, unsure if she knew about the gunfight that had taken place there.

His phone rang. Pulling it from his pocket, he answered Brock's call. "What's up?"

"Get out of there, now! Head south!" Brock shouted. The words barely registered beyond the sound of gunfire.

CHAPTER FOUR

"We have to go!" Steele reached for her hand. Upon hearing gunfire, she'd shoved her feet into the uncomfortable shoes, then grabbed her coat and purse. She barely got one arm inside as Steele led her through the house to the back door, using the same exit strategy as he had at his home.

She wanted to cry as the blisters on her feet burned. The only good news was that when they headed outside, there wasn't a fence to climb.

Small blessings, she thought as she followed Steele through an open backyard to a small tree. Not nearly big enough to provide cover, but she took a moment to release his hand long enough to get her other arm into her winter coat.

"This way." Steele led her on a zigzag path through the stranger's yards. If it wasn't for the danger stalking them, she'd find it funny that they were trespassing once again. And that no one had called the police to report them.

But it wasn't funny to know some gunman wanted her injured or dead. It was completely inconceivable that their safe house had been found so quickly. For a moment, she suspected Brock was working with the bad guys, but then she reminded herself that he'd come to their rescue more than once.

A bare tree branch smacked her in the face, the sharp end nearly poking her in the eye. Focus. She needed to stay alert, not worry about how the safe house had been compromised.

Again!

Her left foot slipped and hit a rock. She cried out in pain. Steele immediately stopped and pulled her close.

"Are you hurt? Are you able to walk?" His terse questions accompanied a steely gaze raking over her.

"I can walk." She felt certain if she couldn't, Steele would try to carry her. Considering her pregnancy, that wasn't an option. She needed Steele to keep her safe, and that meant making sure he could fire his weapon at a potential threat if necessary.

Not lugging her around like a sack of potatoes. A very large and unwieldy sack of potatoes.

Steele nodded, then reached for his radio. "Brock? Where are you?"

"Corner of Latham and Virginia." Brock's voice crackled through the radio. "Where are you?"

Brock led her down a side street. "We're approaching Latham now from Tyndale. I don't know which way Virginia is located."

"I'll come to you." The radio went silent as they continued half walking, half running from the safe house. Her breath sawed from her lungs. She'd never been one for going to the gym but wished more than anything she'd taken up running or biking long before now.

Her lack of physical fitness was holding them back. The

only good news is that the gunman hadn't caught up to them.

At least, not yet.

"I see you," Brock said through the radio. "I'm on your right."

Steele turned to check both ways before crossing the street and heading to the right. When she saw the large SUV rolling toward them, she couldn't hide her relief at getting off her sore feet.

Or her wariness.

When Steele opened the door, she climbed into the back seat. She sent Brock a narrow look. "What happened? How is it that the safe house you rented under your name was found?"

"I don't know." Brock's expression reflected his regret and anger. "You never should have been found, Harper. Never."

"It's not Brock's fault," Steele said calmly. He turned to face her. "But I can see why you're upset."

"My feet are killing me, and I'm worried all this stress from running around will cause me to go into premature labor." She couldn't hold back her condemnation. Maybe it wasn't their fault, but enough was enough already. "This can't keep happening. You must have a dirty cop working for you."

"Not on our team," Steele said. "But you are right to raise the concern. It wasn't that long ago that Reed Carmichael was targeted by a pair of dirty cops."

Somehow, Steele's tone calmed her ragged nerves. She momentarily closed her eyes and took several deep breaths. She needed to get a grip on her emotions. Yelling at these two men who have been risking their lives for her wasn't helpful.

"Check the bag back there," Brock said in a subdued tone. "I got your shoes, socks, and sweatshirt, along with some bandages and a disposable phone. I was heading back to drop them off before grabbing groceries when I saw the brown SUV."

"I'm glad you did," Steele said. "If you hadn't, we may not have gotten away."

"I'm not sure why I came back early," Brock admitted. "I wasn't going to, but then I missed the turn to the grocery store and just kept going."

"I believe that was part of God's plan," she said. "Thanks for the shoes. They mean a lot." Harper tried to smile. Her anger at Brock and Steele was misplaced. They were working for her, not against her.

"I'll call Joe, let him know he really needs to come up with a safe house," Steele said. "And we need to get a replacement vehicle too. Head to the closest rental car agency."

"Will do." Brock hesitated, then said, "Even if Joe can get a safe house approved, it will take time. We might want to consider finding a motel that will take cash."

"We could go to the American Lodge," Steele said thoughtfully. "I know Gary will allow us to pay cash. And he has security cameras."

"I agree. That should work for the interim." Brock gestured to the highway. "There's a rental car agency up ahead."

Harper wasn't sure a rental car was necessary, then again, she hadn't known about the GPS tracker on her sedan either.

"I think it's strange that the gunmen haven't swapped out the brown SUV for something less noticeable," Brock said. "I'm not complaining, but they've been covering their bases really well except for that."

"Good point," Steele agreed. "I don't suppose you got a license plate?"

"There wasn't a front plate," Brock said grimly. "Although I don't think that's against the law anymore."

"Figures." Steele sighed, then turned to look at her as she was opening a pair of socks. "Can you wait a few more minutes? We're about to get a new car. We'll take care of your feet at the motel. I want to make sure we use the antibiotic ointment on your blisters."

She nodded, not willing to risk getting an infection. The pregnancy books she'd gotten from the library hadn't mentioned pregnancy may lower a woman's immune system, but she didn't want to take any chances.

"Here we are." Brock pulled into the parking lot. "Steele, stay here with Harper. I'll be back in a minute."

She tucked her purse inside the bag, clutching it to her chest like a lifeline. When Brock emerged from the building, holding up a key fob, she released her seat belt and pushed out of the back seat. Steele was there, offering a helping hand. She gripped it gratefully.

Walking gingerly, still holding on to the bag, she allowed Steele to escort her to their new vehicle. She wasn't surprised to find they'd arranged for another black SUV.

Was there an unwritten rule that cops had to drive black SUVs?

"Black is one of the most common colors," Steele said, answering the question she hadn't realized she'd said out loud. Steele opened the back passenger door for her. "And they blend in the dark too."

"Makes sense." She slid into the seat, setting the bag beside her. "How far is the American Lodge?"

Brock pulled out of the rental car agency's parking lot as Steele answered. "Ten to fifteen minutes. It's located in Brookland."

She wasn't familiar with Brookland but was glad the motel wasn't too far. The urge to change into comfortable shoes was difficult to ignore. She was worried she'd be forced to go on the run again in the stupid flat dress shoes.

"Whose name did you use on the rental?" Steele asked.

"Joe's." Brock flashed a smile. "He didn't mind, actually spoke to the rental agent personally."

She hoped the change would be enough to shake them loose from the brown SUV. "I still don't understand how we were found at the rental property."

"Yeah, we need to dig into that," Steele agreed with a dark frown. "Joe mentioned the two ATF agents were meeting with Rhy. The fact that we were found so quickly tells me the leak isn't from within the department."

"It's possible my SUV was spotted outside your place, Steele," Brock said. "But tracking my vehicle to the rental property would require access to my credit card."

"Not impossible, considering we don't know who Grotto is working with," Steele mused. "I agree, that's the only option."

She wasn't sure what to think. It wasn't as if she had money to spare, and obviously using her name to secure a motel or a car was out of the question. The gunmen had put a GPS tracker on her car. Clearly, they knew who she was and how to find her.

They rode in silence as Brock navigated the streets. She found herself looking for a brown SUV but didn't see any. When she saw a sign indicating they'd arrived in Brookland, she wanted to weep in gratitude.

Brock turned into the parking lot of the American

Lodge, a two-story white building. She was grateful to be there and reached for the bag. Once again, though, she was instructed to wait while Steele ran inside to arrange their rooms.

Thankfully, it didn't take long. When Steele emerged, he held up two room keys as he jogged over. "We have connecting rooms on the first floor, rooms eleven and twelve."

Sliding out of the back seat, she noticed a room on the second floor directly above their rooms appeared to be boarded up. There was a sign indicating renovations were being done. "I hope the hammering and sawing isn't too loud."

Steele glanced up and shrugged. "I don't hear anything now. I'm sure it will be fine."

The two men walked on either side of her as they crossed the parking lot. Steele unlocked the door of room eleven, then held it for her. She entered the room, pleased to find it was clean and smelled of pine cleaner.

"It's nice, thanks." She dropped onto the bed and kicked off the flats she'd never wear again. After shrugging out of her coat, she stood to head for the bathroom.

"Wait here, I'll bring towels and soap to wash your feet." Steele tossed the key to Brock. "Open the connecting door from the other room, would you? And get the new phone working too."

"Sure." Brock quickly turned and left them alone.

"I can do it," she protested, but Steele ignored her. He unlocked the connecting room door, then hurried into the bathroom. While she waited, she rummaged in the bag for the bandages and antibiotic ointment.

Glancing at her bleeding blisters made her wince. They looked worse than before. When Steele returned, he placed a towel beneath her feet and then gently lifted one foot into a warm soapy towel.

Tears pricked her eyes, and her throat swelled with emotion. She knew Steele was just being nice, that he'd likely have done this to anyone he was trying to protect. Yet his care and concern only emphasized the lack of love in her marriage.

She placed a hand on her rounded belly, reminding herself that God had blessed her with a baby. She couldn't regret her decision to marry Jake, despite everything that had happened.

"How badly do they hurt?" Steele asked. It took her a minute to realize he'd finished with one foot and had started on the other. "We should have picked up some ibuprofen too."

"No need, I'm fine." Her feet would heal in time. "I don't want to take anything other than the prenatal vitamins."

Steele nodded and finished drying her feet. Then he used the antibiotic ointment on the worst blisters and wrapped bandages around them. The simple act of kindness was oddly intimate.

She quickly thrust that thought aside. No point in noticing what a nice, handsome guy Steele was. She wasn't interested. And even if she was, she highly doubted any man would be interested in a pregnant woman or raising a child that wasn't his.

No, there was no point in wishing for what she couldn't have. She would be satisfied with Steele's determination to keep her and the baby safe.

That was all that mattered.

STEELE HAD GLANCED up in time to see Harper's green eyes shine with tears. He hated seeing her cry, yet he was secretly surprised and impressed she hadn't broken down long before now.

He couldn't blame her for getting angry. He wasn't too happy about having to go on the run twice in as many hours. After sliding the thick socks over her feet, he helped her put the new running shoes on.

"Thank you." Her voice was low and hoarse. She blinked again, then rose. "My feet are much better. I'll take care of the towels." Before he could protest, she'd scooped them up and disappeared into the bathroom.

"You're skating a thin line, Delaney," Brock said from the doorway.

He turned to face his teammate. "She's been through a tough time."

"Yeah, sure, you're not getting emotionally involved at all, are you?" Brock didn't bother to hide his sarcasm.

"I only want her to be safe," he insisted. "I'm not interested in replacing Monique in my heart."

"Don't lie to yourself." Brock's tone was curt. "I learned the hard way you can't trust your heart. You need to remember the goal here is to find Tommy Grotto."

Brock was right about their goal. Joe's warning echoed in his mind. "Okay, I hear you. But the answer to finding Tommy Grotto may be drilling down into why they want Harper. And how they're able to track our every move."

Brock sighed and ran a hand over his brown hair. "Yeah. We need food and a computer. I'll call Joe. Maybe he can send Raelyn or one of the others here with supplies."

"Good idea." He glanced over his shoulder, but Harper was still in the bathroom. Deciding to give her some privacy, he crossed the room to join Brock. "Knowing Joe, he'll come

himself. He made it clear he wants to be hands-on, partici-
pating with the team like Rhy."

"Yeah, I know," Brock agreed. "By the way, the new
phone is charging and ready to go."

While his teammate made the call, he paced the length
of the small room. Okay, maybe he was in danger of
becoming too emotionally involved with Harper's plight.
Just because he found it abhorrent that a pregnant woman
would be in danger, nearly kidnapped and shot at, wasn't
the point. Finding the guy responsible was. He needed a
clear head to understand how they kept getting found.

A GPS tracker on Brock's personal vehicle seemed
unlikely. Tracking his credit card to the rental property? Or
tracking their personal phones? That level of sophistication
from Grotto's underlings was concerning.

"Thanks, Joe." Brock slid his phone into his pocket.
"He's on his way and is picking up Sammy's sub sandwiches for lunch."

"Lunch?" Harper's voice had him turning toward the
connecting door. She looked adorable wearing the oversized
sweatshirt and running shoes. The forest green of the sweatshirt matched her eyes.

"Have you had Sammy's subs?" he asked. "They're
great."

"I have, yes." Her brow furrowed. "Trent sometimes
orders them for the office."

He could tell she was concerned about keeping her job,
and he didn't know how to reassure her one way or the
other. Especially since it didn't seem that they were going to
find the gunmen anytime soon.

"Why don't you sit down?" Steele went over to pull out
one of the chairs around the small table. "Keep the pressure
off your feet."

"I can't tell you how grateful I am to have decent shoes and socks." She dropped into the chair. "At least now I won't slow us down as much if we need to go on the run again."

"Hopefully, it won't come to that." He scowled, not liking the idea of the gunmen showing up here. Bad enough that the room above them had been shot up last month by a crazed gunman trying to kill Elly Finnegan. The near miss had him crossing to the door and opening it to verify the camera was pointing in the correct position.

"I checked too," Brock said with a lopsided grin. "Figured we need to be on high alert."

"Checked what?" Harper asked.

"The positions of the security cameras." He smiled reassuringly. "Don't worry, everything is fine. You're safe here." Stress probably wasn't good for the baby. And he was more than capable of worrying enough for the both of them.

"Per his text message, Joe is five minutes out." Brock glanced up from his phone. "My stomach is growling loud enough for him to hear it."

"You're hungry? We're the ones who have been burning up calories running from one location to the next," Steele protested.

"And I'm eating for two," Harper added.

"Are you really trying to out-hunger me?" Brock demanded.

"Yeah, pretty much." He winked at Harper who blushed. She was so beautiful his heart ached. But he forced himself to keep his tone light. "Harper wins; she gets first dibs on the sandwiches."

"I can't argue with a pregnant woman," Brock groused.

Five minutes later, he noticed a familiar vehicle pulling

into the parking lot. "Joe's here." He crossed to the window to peer out, then opened the door.

"Hey, the repairs are looking good," Joe said, nodding at the second-floor room as he slid out from behind the wheel. He reached in and grabbed a computer-carrying case along with a large bag of food.

"Any idea when they'll be finished?" Steele asked, opening the door wider.

"Windows are going in next week. I should know since I paid for them." Joe handed him the bag.

"Why on earth would you pay for windows?" Harper asked.

"Ah, well, it was partially my fault the room was damaged." Joe set the computer case on the floor. "Rhy is splitting the cost."

"Your fault?" Harper glanced between the three men. "You were on a case?"

"Yes. But like I said, you don't need to worry." Steele quickly unpacked the sandwiches, desperate to change the subject. "You pick first, Harper."

She scanned the sub labels, then chose a grilled chicken sub. "Thanks."

There was more than enough to go around. He noticed Harper bowed her head for a long moment.

"I'd like to say grace," Joe said.

Harper glanced up in surprise, then nodded.

He and Brock bowed their heads as their boss prayed. "Dear Lord Jesus, we thank You for this food we are about to eat. We ask that You continue to keep Harper and her baby safe in Your care. Amen."

"Amen." He spoke without hesitation.

"Amen." Harper cleared her throat. "I'd like to add a prayer for your safety too." She glanced at him, then at

Brock, and finally Joe. "For all of you putting your lives on the line for me."

"Amen." Brock arched a brow. "Although that is the job we signed up for. You know, the slogan on our squad is to protect and serve."

Steele knew his buddy was trying to make a point. And by the knowing look in Joe's eye, he suspected his boss agreed.

He took a bite of his roast beef sandwich. "How was the meeting between the ATF guys and Rhy? Did we learn anything useful?"

"Not really." Joe grimaced. "Sounds like they did get one crate of guns after the warehouse shooting but had expected more."

One crate of guns was better than none, but he silently agreed that there should have been more. "I wonder if they had already cleared out some of the weapons before we arrived on scene."

"That's the general consensus," Joe admitted. "Rhy isn't happy, and the ATF guys aren't either."

"They must have some leads they're following up on," Steele pressed. "I have a feeling they're holding back."

"All I know is that they're still searching for Tommy Grotto, Ellis Starkey, and Waylon Brooks," Joe said. "They seem to think arresting those three guys will bring down the entire operation."

"What about the three dead guys?" Brock asked. "Did we get their names?"

Joe glanced at Harper. Steele noticed, and added, "It may help to see if Harper recognizes their names. I only put mug shots together of the three top suspects. I didn't have IDs on those guys to add them to the list."

"Okay, yes. We have names," Joe said. "Arlo Carbine, Kenny Dillon and Perro Segura."

Steele watched Harper's face closely, but there was no sign of recognition in her expression.

"I'm sorry. Those names don't sound familiar." She set her half-eaten sub down. "I wish I could be more help."

"Hey, it's okay," he quickly assured her. "We know you're doing your best."

"We have street names too," Joe said. "Carbo, Dillweed, and Parrott."

"Parrott?" Harper's eyes widened as she latched onto that name. "I may have seen his name on a text message. I assumed it was one of the guys working at the warehouse. But that was a long time ago." She glanced at her rounded stomach, and added, "It's been over seven months since I was with Jake."

"It's a connection," Joe said. "I appreciate you letting us know."

Just linking her ex-husband to one of the dead guys wasn't really enough, but Steele agreed with Joe that every bit of intel counted. The ATF guys, Bryon Perkins or Steve Banner, could possibly use that information to get more out of Jake Feldman.

He was glad when Harper resumed eating. They ate in silence for a moment. Talking about dead guys and gunmen was something cops did without paying much attention, but not Harper. As if by tactic agreement, they let her finish her meal in peace.

When Joe's phone rang, breaking the silence, she jumped. Then flushed with embarrassment.

"It's Raelyn," Joe said, before pressing the speaker button so they could all listen in. "What's up?"

"We just got a report of a dead body in a dumpster,"

Raelyn said. "Grayson and I decided to tag along since the location is three-quarters of a mile from the warehouse."

Steele's stomach clenched. "Who is it?"

"He's been here for a while, but I'm pretty sure the vic is Ellis Starkey. He was shot execution style at close range to the back of his head."

Harper gasped and paled. He exchanged a grim look with Joe and Brock. Was Tommy Grotto getting rid of loose ends?

And was that the reason they were coming after Harper?

CHAPTER FIVE

Ellis Starkey was dead. A chill snaked down her spine at the news. Harper knew his decision to buy and sell guns with Jake had been responsible for this outcome. Yet Ellis had always been decent to her. In some respects, he'd been nicer to her than Jake had been.

Especially toward the end of their marriage. It was as if Ellis felt bad for what Jake was putting her through. She remembered how he'd brought her a large blue vase, allegedly from the warehouse. There was a small chip on one side, which Starkey said was the reason they couldn't sell it.

For some odd reason, she'd taken the vase with her to the apartment. Every morning she walked in Greenland Park before work, gathering wildflowers. Placing them in the vase every few days had brightened the otherwise dingy apartment. Looking back, she understood that Ellis and Jake must have sold some legitimate items, along with the guns.

Steele's voice interrupted her thoughts. "Any other evidence, Rae?"

"Hang on, we're checking." There was a long pause with muted voices in the background. "Yes, looks like Starkey's head was down, like with his chin to his chest, when he was shot. Appears as if the slug might still be inside the body. The ME just rolled up; we should know more in a few hours."

"Okay, thanks for that and keep us in the loop." Joe reached over to end the call.

Steele's gaze searched her face. "Are you okay?"

She shrugged. "I know Ellis was a criminal, just like Jake. But he was always nice to me. I hate knowing he died with someone pressing a gun to the back of his head."

"I understand." Steele glanced at Joe and Brock. "Unfortunately, that's the risk you take hanging out with criminals."

"I don't condone what he did." She sighed and rubbed her hands over her stomach. "I just feel bad about his death. I always had the impression that Jake dragged Ellis into the illegal gun business."

"Everyone has a choice," Joe said quietly. "He could have refused, or he could have gone to the police."

Joe and Steele were right. Logically she understood Ellis had made his choice. And paid for that decision with his life.

"You mentioned your ex may have dragged Starkey into a life of crime," Brock said. "What exactly do you remember?"

She grimaced, wishing she'd just kept her mouth shut. "There was nothing specific. But the few times I saw them together, Jake came across as the leader. Ellis seemed to be along for the ride."

"Did you ever visit their warehouses?" Joe asked.

"No, but I knew where they were." Why did it suddenly feel like she was being interrogated again? "I told you I had no idea they were buying and selling guns. How could I? I honestly thought they were buying stuff wholesale and turning it around for a profit. It wasn't as if Jake confided in me." She hesitated, then added, "I will say that the last six months of our marriage were the worst. Maybe that's when the gun business started. It almost seemed as if Jake wanted to get rid of me."

"Get rid of you, how?" Steele asked with a frown.

"Not killing me, but he didn't want me hanging around. Although he wasn't happy to find out I was leaving either." She shook her head, feeling helpless. It was difficult to put those troubled times between her and Jake into words. "Looking back, I think he was angry about my leaving because it was my decision, not his."

Steele nodded. "That would make sense."

She appreciated him trying to smooth things over. "I've told you everything I know. I remember a text from Parrott; it only caught my eye because of the odd name. I knew Ellis and Jake were in business together, but I assumed it was legit."

"Look, we believe you," Steele said, shooting Brock a pointed look. "But any small detail you can remember could help us find the people responsible for shooting Starkey and coming after you."

"I'll keep trying, but I was focused more on my failing marriage than on what Ellis and Jake were doing with the business." That was the truth. At first, she'd blamed herself, then realized she wasn't responsible for Jake's actions. He was. And that's when she began scrimping and saving to leave him.

"You mentioned the last six months of your marriage," Joe said. "Can you pinpoint anything that Jake said or did that might indicate he'd gone into a life of crime?"

Sitting back in her seat, she forced herself to remember those days she'd begun to realize Jake wasn't the man she'd married. His attitude had changed, and he was quick to anger. A memory came to her. "I remember finding a wad of cash in his pocket. He'd left his jeans on the floor, and I was going to toss them in the laundry. Jake roughly grabbed the money from my hand, bending back my fingers in the process. We didn't have a lot of extra cash, and we had a credit card bill that was coming due, so I asked him to give me some of the money to pay it. He refused, claiming he and Ellis had made a cash deal but that he owed some people for products that were about to be shipped, so the money wasn't really ours. When I pressed further about the credit card bill, he said he'd take care of it. He did, so I let it go."

"Do you know how much money he had?" Joe asked.

"No, but I saw a one-hundred-dollar bill on the outside of the wad of money. I assumed they were all hundreds, but he caught me before I could count them."

"And when was this?" Brock asked.

"Maybe three months before I left him." It was early January now; she'd discovered she was pregnant in August. "Maybe April or May? I honestly can't say for sure."

"Okay, that's helpful." Steele smiled reassuringly. "Just keep thinking back over that period of time, Harper. If anything else comes to you, let us know."

Hadn't she already promised to do that? She tried not to show her frustration. She knew the men sitting around her wanted to help. That they wanted to keep her safe.

She imagined Ellis being shot and killed and tossed into the dumpster. Her anger dissipated. "I will." She reached into her pocket, belatedly remembering she'd left her phone behind at Steele's house. "I—uh, should check in with my boss."

"Again?" Steele asked with a frown.

"I can't afford to lose my job," she shot back. "I need to be able to support myself and my baby."

"Here, use this replacement phone." Brock handed her a small, cheap phone. "I wrote the number down for you."

"Thanks." She rose to her feet, then moved into the connecting room for some privacy. Maybe she didn't need to call in, but the fact was that she craved some sense of normalcy. Her job was important to her. She hadn't been kidding about needing her job to support herself. She dialed her boss's number, but he didn't answer. No doubt because he didn't recognize the number. She left a brief message, letting him know she'd lost her phone and was using this number temporarily.

She sat on the edge of the bed for a moment, taking slow, deep breaths. It didn't seem fair that Ellis was dead while Jake was alive and being protected by ATF agents. In her heart, she wished it was the opposite. God would want her to forgive Jake and to let go of her anger and resentment.

She silently promised to do better. Really, as long as Jake wasn't a part of her life, she didn't care what he did with his second chance at freedom. Hopefully, he'd learn from his mistakes.

When her phone rang, she startled badly. So much for trying to relax and remain calm. Every sound had her jumping out of her skin. She answered the phone, recognizing her boss's number. "Hi, Trent."

"Harper, I've been trying to get in touch with you!" He

sounded agitated, as if she'd lost her phone on purpose to inconvenience him.

"I'm sorry. You can reach me at this number from now on."

"Yeah, okay," he said absently. "I called because I need to find the witness file on the Otterson case. I've looked all over but can't find it." There was a hint of panic in his tone. "You didn't lose it, did you?"

"No, of course not. I've been keeping all the Otterson files in the bottom right-hand drawer of my desk. It's locked, but you have a key, don't you?" She frowned, wondering if her boss was losing it. He was the one who'd directed her to keep the Otterson files under lock and key. She'd done exactly as he'd asked.

"Oh, yeah, that's right. Hang on, let me see if it's there." She could hear rummaging sounds, then the snick of a drawer opening. "It's here. I found it." Trent sounded almost giddy with relief. "Thanks, Harper."

Before she could say anything in response, he disconnected from the call. She lowered the phone to her lap, frowning at the strange call. Maybe Trent was struggling because she helped keep the office running smoothly and efficiently when she was there. It was one of the things Trent had complimented her on. Under normal circumstances, she'd have been there, handing him the files he'd need for the day according to his schedule. As things changed throughout the day, she anticipated his needs then too.

Yet it still seemed odd that he hadn't thought to check the locked desk drawer for the witness file. Neil Otterson had been their top-paying client over the past few months. She'd noticed the increasing billable hours, which made sense as they were preparing for trial.

It occurred to her that she'd never asked what crime Neil Otterson had been charged with.

The reasons for their clients needing a criminal defense lawyer weren't really any of her business. She didn't care, and in some cases, she would rather not know. Trent Gibson and Earl Roberts liked to keep their client's business private too. It was the foundation for attorney/client privilege.

"Harper?" Steele's voice came from the doorway connecting their rooms.

She glanced up. "Yes?"

"Who were you talking to?" Steele stepped closer. "I'm not trying to be nosy, but that's a new phone. I'm surprised anyone has the number to call you."

"I called my boss to let him know how to reach me." She rose to her feet. "Trent returned my call because he was looking for a specific file. I highly doubt his upcoming trial is related to the danger stalking me."

"Oh yeah, he's a criminal defense attorney." Steele's gaze was thoughtful. "Who is his client?"

She hesitated. "I'm not sure I'm supposed to tell you."

"I don't think the name of a client is a secret," he said. "Usually those charged with crimes are listed on the Wisconsin Circuit Court database with the name of their attorney representing them. Anyone can find out that information."

"Only if you know the client's name, though," she protested. Was he right? Maybe the name of a client being represented by an attorney wasn't a secret.

"I can probably run a report on all cases where Trent Gibson is listed as the defense attorney," he responded.

He probably could. She sighed. "He has several clients, but his biggest case is for a client named Neil Otterson. I have no idea what he's been charged with, but I know he's out on bail. I figured it can't be too serious if he's walking around on the streets of the city."

"Otterson?" Steele frowned. "We should probably check into him, just to be sure."

"Go ahead." She was suddenly weary of all this talk of criminals. Her ex-husband, Ellis Starkey, and now Otterson.

She closed her eyes and prayed for peace. Especially for her unborn child.

STEELE FELT bad for grilling Harper about her boss's client, but he hadn't liked hearing that she'd called the guy. Logically, he knew Trent Gibson wasn't a suspect.

But he did represent criminals. The name Neil Otterson sounded familiar. It took him a moment to place the name with the headline.

The guy had been charged with first-degree murder of two young Hispanic men during what he alleged was a carjacking. The suspects had been shot outside Otterson's vehicle located in a deserted parking lot, and there had been no evidence of an attempted carjacking, which was why the DA had filed murder charges. Both men had been unarmed too. Otterson shouldn't be out on bond, but that's what happened when you had big bucks. If he remembered correctly, Otterson had a previous felony conviction for drug dealing, but it had been several years ago. Since no drugs had been found on the scene of the shooting, and the two dead men didn't have drug connections, the judge had deemed that felony conviction to be outside the scope of the current case.

Even though having a felony conviction meant Otterson shouldn't have had a gun in the first place. Last he'd heard, Otterson was working under the theory of self-defense.

With the help of his lawyer, Trent Gibson.

"I know what you're thinking," Harper said. "Otterson isn't involved in this."

Since that was what he'd been thinking, he couldn't help but smile. "The thought crossed my mind."

"Even if Neil Otterson was upset at how Trent was handling his case, he wouldn't come after me. Trent has a wife and two kids."

"Yeah, okay." It bothered Steele to know Harper was working for a defense attorney, even though it shouldn't. Difficult to imagine a carjacking was related to a gunrunning operation, so he let it go. He didn't need to go down a completely different rabbit hole.

His goal, and that of the entire team, had to be finding and arresting Tommy Grotto. That was the only way to keep Harper safe.

"Steele?"

He glanced back to see Brock standing there. "Yeah?"

"We're hitting the road." Brock gave him a stern look, as if warning him to stay cool. "Joe is going to leave his SUV here for you. The keys are on the table."

"Thanks." He tried not to feel left out of the investigation. "Keep me updated, okay?"

"Sure thing." Brock glanced over to where Harper was sitting on the edge of the bed. It looked as if he might say something more, but he turned away. Brock and Joe took off, leaving him and Harper alone.

"I have work to do." Leaving Harper alone wasn't easy, but he turned to sit at the table. After booting up the computer, he did a quick search on Neil Otterson. It appeared the guy's trial was scheduled to begin in two weeks. Sooner than he would have anticipated, since even insisting on a speedy trial took upward of eight to ten months.

Not important. Unless, of course, Otterson had purchased his gun illegally from Feldman. Yet even if he had, that wouldn't explain why a guy who'd shot two men in alleged self-defense would come after Harper now.

He forced himself to concentrate on the matter at hand. As he was still in the Wisconsin Circuit Court database, he entered Ellis Starkey's name.

Starkey had no criminal record either.

When he entered Jacob Feldman's name, he was surprised to see the guy had a prior burglary conviction. Nothing more serious, though. It was a stretch to go from robbing someone to buying and selling guns.

He wondered if Harper had known about Feldman's past burglary arrest. Then he decided it didn't matter. She had moved on, filing for divorce just before Feldman had been arrested. Sitting back in the chair, he mentally reviewed what little he knew about the guy's arrest. Hadn't Banner and Perkins mentioned an anonymous tip claiming Feldman's business not being legit?

Had Starkey made that call? If so, it would also explain why the guy had been murdered execution style. A warning to any others who might be involved not to try the same thing.

Since the anonymous call had come through a burner phone, bought with cash from a place that didn't have security cameras, the source had been a dead end.

Like Starkey himself was dead.

Giving himself a mental shake, he tried to think of another avenue to pursue. His thoughts kept coming back to the two ATF agents, Steve Banner and Bryon Perkins.

There was no reason to suspect either of them of being dirty. He was letting the recent events mess with his head.

They'd been found at his place by a tracking device on Harper's car. Or her phone.

Probably both.

But that didn't explain how they'd been found so quickly at the rental property. Even if he wanted to suspect the ATF agents, they didn't know where they were staying.

Yet the ATF could easily assume that the rental would be under his name or Brock's.

With a sigh, he stood and closed the computer. He moved into the doorway between their rooms as Harper bent and picked up her flat dress shoes.

"You want me to toss them for you?" he asked.

"I just noticed a bump inside." She began poking at the interior of one shoe. "The same spot where I ended up with a bad blister."

"A crack in the sole?"

She ruthlessly pulled the bottom insert out. A small flat disk came flying out with it. His gaze widened as the implication sank deep.

Another tracking device?

"Let me see that." He scooped it up, his blood running cold when he saw the fine lines threaded through it. Then he tossed it into the garbage near the desk in her room. "We need to get out of here."

"And go where?" To her credit, Harper didn't argue as she reached for her coat.

Using his radio, he called Brock. "We found another tracker in Harper's shoe. I need you and Joe to turn around to come back here ASAP!"

"On our way," Brock said.

His next call was to Gary Campbell. "Keep your eye on those cameras. We're expecting company."

"Got it," Gary said.

"Shouldn't we leave now?" Harper asked, standing beside him. "Should I leave my purse too?"

"Yes. Drop the purse with everything inside next to the shoes. Toss your coat too. We won't leave until we have backup in place." He offered her his coat, then hunkered near the window. He didn't have a wide enough view of their surroundings but trusted that Gary would pick up anyone creeping toward them via his cameras.

Hopefully in time to prevent another shoot-out like the one that had taken place last month with Elly as the target. They really had to stop using Gary's place as a hideout. The poor guy was getting far more than he'd bargained for.

His phone rang. Seeing Gary's name, his gut clenched. "What do you have?"

"Movement from behind the trees directly across from room eleven," Gary said. "Should I call the police?"

"Yes." Room eleven was Harper's room. Where the disk was located. They were currently in room twelve, which was the last room in the row, partially hidden behind the staircase.

Before he could say anything more, there was a loud crack as the window of Harper's motel room shattered. Instantly, smoke began to fill the air.

A smoke bomb designed the flush them outside and directly into the line of fire.

"Shut the connecting door!" He lifted the window enough to poke the barrel of his gun through and fired off a warning round. Harper coughed as she shut the door.

"My eyes are burning," she whispered. "I hope the smoke doesn't harm the baby."

"Grab the sheets from the bed, jam them along the bottom of the door. Then come kneel behind me." He kept his gaze focused outside. Where was Brock's SUV? He didn't know how far away Brock and Joe had gotten. But based on the shooter being outside, there wasn't a second to spare.

They needed backup now!

He found himself praying the Brookland cops would show up before the shooter began peppering the hotel room windows.

Seeing movement within the trees across the parking lot, he fired off another warning round. He hoped the shooter didn't know they had connecting rooms.

As soon as the thought crossed his mind, a bullet penetrated the glass above his head.

Harper cried out in fear, cowering behind him. He fired two more rounds in the direction where he'd last seen movement.

Harper began softly praying, begging God to keep her baby safe from harm. He couldn't let himself be distracted by her fear. He'd been in worse situations than this. He only needed to hold the shooter off long enough for Brock to get there.

Piece of cake.

"Hold your fire," Brock's voice crackled through the radio. "I'm coming in on foot."

"Roger, but shooter is stationed directly across from our rooms. Watch your six."

"I see him." He figured Brock had binoculars trained on the wooded area. He and Brock were both very familiar with the area. "I'm going to draw his fire. When I do that, I want you and Harper to get out of there."

"No, we can't," Harper whispered. "He'll see us!"

"Are you sure there's not more than one shooter out there?" Steele asked.

"Joe is moving along the back of the motel. He hasn't reported seeing anyone else," Brock said. "He'll meet you on the side closest to the staircase."

"Okay, we'll get ready to run." He turned to look at Harper. "We only need to get outside and around the corner where Joe will be waiting. I'll go first, you stay behind me."

"It's too dangerous." Her red eyes were swollen, and tears streaked down her cheeks. How much was from the smoke or from their current dicey situation, he wasn't sure.

Another bullet pierced the glass to his right.

"We can't stay here. Just trust me, okay?" He turned to watch through the window. He couldn't see Brock getting into position but imagined he'd station himself near the lobby.

"Now!" Brock said, and opened fire.

Steele jumped up and wrenched open the door. Despite her protests, Harper followed right behind him, clutching the back of his bullet-resistant vest. He fired toward the trees, too, then quickly shifted so that Harper could get around the corner safely. Then he quickly ducked and followed.

"This way," Joe urged. Steele didn't argue, following his boss's lead as they ran along the back of the building. He didn't see an SUV. Brock and Joe must have hidden it somewhere nearby.

The sound of gunfire didn't let up. Steele knew Brock was doing his best to keep the shooter busy, enabling them to escape.

Then there was nothing but silence. Joe finally stopped and looked at him. "The Finnegan homestead is about ten to twelve blocks away. Take Harper there and wait for us. I'm going back to help Brock."

He didn't like leaving his teammates behind. But he didn't have a choice. He watched Joe jog back the way they'd come, then forced himself to keep going.

The best thing he could do for Joe and Brock now was get Harper to safety.

CHAPTER SIX

Harper's stomach knotted with tension. She couldn't believe Tommy Grotto's men had planted a tracking device in her shoe. And maybe one in her purse too. Steele had even instructed her to leave her coat behind. Yet knowing exactly how they'd kept getting found was reassuring. Now that they'd left those awful shoes, her purse, and coat behind, she felt certain they'd be safe wherever they went.

What had Joe said? They were heading to the Finnegan homestead? She assumed that meant Rhy's home, but she wasn't sure.

Her feet were much better in the running shoes, making it easy to keep up with Steele's long stride as they ducked through one set of backyards and then another.

Well, a little easier. She was still carrying extra weight with being pregnant and admittedly out of shape. At least her feet didn't slip and slide as easily on the snowy grass. She knew from Steele's frequent glances back at her that he was trying to move at a pace she could easily maintain.

He stopped near a house that was completely dark. Grateful for the rest, she struggled to control her breathing.

She'd never run so much in her entire life as she had since this nightmare started.

She decided she hated running. Despised everything about it. Maybe she'd feel better if she wasn't seven months pregnant, but she doubted it.

"Are you feeling okay?" Steele asked, his voice a husky whisper near her ear. "No problems with the baby?"

"I'm fine." She rested one hand on her abdomen. The baby wasn't moving at the moment, but she'd been sure to monitor activity the way her obstetrician had suggested. "Baby is fine too."

His gaze held hers. Then he gave her hand a gentle squeeze. "We're about halfway there."

Only halfway? She swallowed a groan. If anyone had asked, she'd have said they'd been running for miles. She drew in another deep breath and forced herself to nod. "I'm ready when you are."

He flashed a reassuring smile. Grateful to have Steele at her side through all of this, she pushed away from the wall of the house and followed him out toward the street. Of course, Steele didn't stay on the road for long, he once again cut through the narrow space between two houses.

She wasn't nervous about cutting through people's private property anymore. It seemed as if no one cared that they were trespassing. They approached another house when suddenly a large dog charged from the shadows, barking madly.

"Steele!" She reared away from the animal, throwing her hands up to protect her face. She tripped over the raised edge of a flower bed and almost hit the ground. She braced herself to feel the dog's teeth sinking into her body.

"It's okay, this way." Steele drew her close and eased away from the animal. Stunned she hadn't been attacked, she stared at the large black dog. Belatedly realizing there was a long chain attached to his collar.

Her heart was thundering in her chest like a high-speed train. She couldn't breathe, couldn't seem to get her fear under control. The dog continued to bark and lunge toward them as far as his chain would allow.

"Brutus, shut up!" a loud voice shouted from the house.

Brutus? Fitting name for a dog that likely would have torn her limb from limb.

"I want to go home." The words escaped from her mouth before she could stop them.

"You can't go home, Harper." Steele continued pushing forward, hauling her with him. He was right. Of course, she couldn't go home.

But she didn't want to keep running from gunmen either.

"Two more blocks," Steele murmured. "You can do it."

"Yeah, if I don't have a heart attack." She ran for a few minutes, then added, "That dog scared the stuffing out of me."

"I know, I wasn't expecting that either." Steele slowed his pace. "See that house through the trees? The one with the lights on upstairs?"

"Yes."

"That's the homestead." He dropped to a walk, glancing both ways before heading to the corner and walking on the road. As they approached the property from the front, he pulled out his cell phone. She heard the sound of ringing, then a male voice answered. "Steele? Where are you?"

"Out front." She saw movement near the window. Steele raised his hand and waved. "If you don't want us to come inside, we can sit out back to wait for Joe and Brock."

"Don't be ridiculous. Come up to the door." The call

ended. Steele pocketed his phone and drew her along with him toward the brightly lit front porch.

They'd barely stepped onto the porch when the front door swung open. A tall man with blond hair stood before her. About as tall as Steele, but maybe not quite as broad across the shoulders. "Come in."

"Thanks, Rhy." Steele nudged her forward. "Sorry to bring danger to the homestead."

"It's okay. I'm just glad you're not hurt." Rhy smiled at her. "Ms. Crane, I'm Rhyland Finnegan. That's my wife, Devon, and our daughter, Colleen."

She'd noticed the pretty dark-haired woman sitting on the sofa, cradling a baby in her arms. Seeing the young infant made her realize why Steele had apologized for bringing danger to their doorstep. "It's nice to meet you, please call me Harper." She frowned, then added, "We shouldn't stay. I didn't realize you had a young baby here."

"We won't be here long," Steele said. "And we found that tracker in your shoe, so we should be in the clear."

"In her shoe?" Rhy's brow arched. "That's a weird spot to plant one."

"Tell me about it." Steele frowned. "There may have been one in her purse too. We didn't bother to check, just left it behind with the shoes. And her coat for extra measure. The running shoes she's wearing are new, as is the sweatshirt."

"That's good," Rhy agreed.

She tried not to gape at the beautiful interior of the Finnegan home. It was huge, bigger than any other house she'd ever seen. She wished she could sit beside Devon to talk about pregnancy and babies. She hadn't had the ability to talk to other young mothers since her last church meeting.

"Come sit beside me, Harper." As if reading her mind, Devon patted the sofa. "Looks like you need to get off your feet for a while."

"Thanks." She sat on the edge. "Colleen is beautiful. How old is she?"

"She'll be three months old in another week." Devon smiled. "We have been blessed with a wonderful baby. She doesn't quite sleep through the night, but she's made it five hours, which is amazing."

It was hard for Harper to take her eyes off the baby. It was all too easy to imagine holding her own child the same way.

"Harper?" Rhy's voice drew her attention. "Can you help us understand how anyone was able to get into your apartment to plant the tracking device in your shoe?"

She frowned. "I have no idea. I can't stand knowing someone had been in my apartment when I wasn't there."

"Tell us about your routine," Steele suggested. "Other than working Monday through Friday at the law office."

"I often work from home on Fridays," she corrected. "And I grocery shop on Saturday mornings and attend church on Sunday. Sometimes I attend church meetings after our services, but lately I've been too tired."

"So anyone watching you for a week or two would know when it was safe to sneak inside," Rhy said.

"Without a key?" She found that difficult to believe. "How would anyone get in?"

"Many of those older buildings aren't as secure as they should be," Steele said. "I've seen your eight-family building from the outside. I don't think it would take much effort to gain access to your apartment."

That was a horrifying thought. Yet there also wasn't much she could do about it. She couldn't afford to move. For all she knew, she might not have a job once this mess was over.

Not that Trent Gibson would be cavalier about letting her go. But she needed to get back to work as soon as possible.

"This makes me wonder if my clothes have devices sewn into them." She looked down. "Although I'm only wearing my own slacks at this point."

"You know, I have plenty of maternity clothes. We're about the same size," Devon said. "Rhy, hold the baby, will you? Harper, come with me. We'll get you set up with more comfortable clothes in no time."

"Oh, really, that's not necessary," she protested.

"Yes, it is. Please let me help." Devon smiled. "I want you to feel comfortable."

"Okay." She gave in, partially because it seemed rude to keep refusing. And because she genuinely liked Devon. "Thank you."

The second floor was full of bedrooms and bathrooms. Devon pulled out several maternity outfits, and there was one in particular in cream and green colors that looked soft and warm. When Harper ducked into the master bathroom, she checked her underwear for anything unusual but didn't find anything. After changing into the borrowed clothes, she instantly felt better. Maybe it was psychological, shedding her dress maternity slacks for something nicer. Or maybe it was just being the recipient of Devon's kindness.

Tears pricked her eyelids, and she grabbed a tissue. Her hormones were completely out of whack these days. She'd never been a crier until recently. Time to pull herself together. She stepped out of the bathroom. "Thanks, Devon. This is sweet of you."

"You look adorable." Devon smiled. "I'm happy to help. Do you want another change of clothes for the road?"

"No, this is fine." She wouldn't be greedy. "Thanks so much. I thought the large sweatshirt would be fine, but it didn't really fit right."

"I thought the same thing during my pregnancy. Extra-large only works in the early months. And maternity clothes are much cuter." Devon turned and led the way back down-stairs. "Try not to worry. I know Steele, Joe, and the rest of the tactical team will continue to keep you safe."

Her throat closed with emotion, knowing she was right. She was alive only because Steele, Brock, and Joe had been there.

The sound of a baby crying reached her ears. Rhy was swaying from side to side with Colleen in his arms. "Hey, it's okay. Mommy's here."

"Aw, is she getting hungry?" Devon crossed to her husband. Rhy wrapped his arm around her shoulders, bringing her in for a sweet kiss.

"She is." Rhy chuckled. "Impatient young lady."

Devon laughed and eased the baby from his arms. Rhy kissed her again, and Harper had to tear her gaze away from the love radiating between the couple.

Her heart aching for something she'd never have.

———

STEELE DIDN'T KNOW the source of sadness in Harper's gaze, but when his phone pinged with a text from Joe, he quickly read it out loud. "The shooter escaped."

"Not good." Rhy frowned, his gaze briefly following his wife as she headed upstairs with the baby. Then he turned to face Steele. "I was hoping that Gary's cameras would help us grab him."

"They're primarily focused on protecting the building and occupants, not the entire property." Steele grimaced. "Although I was hoping we'd get him too."

"I don't understand," Harper spoke up. "How did he get away?"

"It's hard to chase a gunman when he's shooting." Steele sighed. "Maybe if Joe hadn't had to get us out of there, they could have gotten to him."

"So it's my fault." Harper's tone was full of regret.

"No, it's the gunman's fault." Rhy dug into his pocket, producing a set of car keys. "I think you should take my SUV. I can hitch a ride to work in the morning with one of the guys. I'd rather you have a set of wheels."

"Are you sure?" He caught the key fob Rhy tossed to him. "We can try another rental tomorrow."

"Just use my SUV for now," Rhy said. His gaze darted to Harper. "Are you sure you're not hurt? Baby is okay?"

"I'm not hurt." Harper's smile didn't reach her eyes. "Nothing a little rest and sleep won't cure."

"Yeah, I've had her running a lot over the past day and a half," Steele admitted. "We need another place to stay. Not here," he hastily added. "Maybe another hotel."

"How about the City Central Hotel downtown?" Rhy pulled out his phone. "I can call and arrange for a suite. They're on the ground floor, down the hall from the lobby."

"You sound as if you've spent a lot of time there," Harper said.

Rhy barked out a laugh. "You could say that. Our family has used it as a refuge several times over the past year."

Steele didn't want to admit that Elly had been found there just last month. The same way she'd been found at the

American Lodge. Was it a mistake to go to the same place? He wasn't sure, except they had found the tracking device. Harper didn't have her phone, her purse, her shoes, or her coat. She was wearing all new, albeit borrowed, clothing.

He didn't see how they could be tracked to the City Central Hotel. He curled his fingers around the keys. "Thanks, Rhy. If you could arrange for a suite, I'd be grateful."

"Consider it done." Rhy scrolled through his phone, then turned away to make the call.

"I'm glad we're not staying here," Harper said in a low tone. "I would never forgive myself if Devon and Colleen were in danger."

"I wasn't going to let that happen either," he assured her. It was bad enough knowing Harper was pregnant. Keeping mom and baby safe was proving far more difficult than he'd anticipated. "We'll hit the road soon."

"I thought Joe and Brock were meeting us here?" She tipped her head to the side. "And why do they call it the homestead?"

"The Finnegan home has always been called that; it was a nickname their parents used." He sent a quick response to Joe. "Joe and Brock will be tied up at the scene for a while anyway. They can meet us at the hotel later."

"Okay, that's fine." She ran her fingers through her blond hair. "It would be nice to feel safe."

Her words were like a punch in the gut. No woman should be in constant danger like this.

His sister Amelia's face flashed in his mind. He thrust it aside with an effort.

"All set," Rhy said, returning to the living room. "Drive safe and watch your tail."

"Will do. Thanks again." He led the way to the door

leading to the garage, then glanced over his shoulder. "I'll check in with you tomorrow, okay?"

"Call anytime." Rhy's expression was solemn. "We need to get to the bottom of this."

He couldn't agree more. Rhy disarmed the alarm so they could get out to the SUV. After waiting for Harper to get settled in the passenger seat, he opened the garage door and drove down the driveway.

There was a long silence as he headed to the closest freeway ramp. After ten minutes, Harper said, "I never heard of the City Central Hotel."

"It's located near the courthouse." He glanced at her. "The ADAs use it for witnesses sometimes."

"I'm not a witness." She stared down at her hands folded in her lap. "Isn't that why I didn't qualify for a safe house?"

"You're not a material witness, but I think Rhy will talk to our assistant chief tomorrow, see if he can't change his mind." He wanted to reassure her that she was safe, but really, they'd barely escaped the American Lodge.

"I understand. I read the news; there's a lot of crime. The city can't put everyone in a safe house."

Yeah, that much was true. And it wasn't as if she had any key evidence to provide in the case that would warrant placing her in a safe house paid for by the city.

The trip to the hotel didn't take long. He parked near the side entrance, but then walked around to enter the lobby. Thanks to Rhy's call, the clerk had their keys ready to go.

The suite at City Central was nicer than the American Lodge, but it wasn't anything super fancy. Still, Harper looked around in awe.

"This is great. I feel like I'm living in luxury." Her brow furrowed. "I'll never be able to repay you."

"Not necessary, we've got it covered." The suite was far from luxurious. Just thinking about her tenuous situation bothered him. Why did he feel the need to support her financially? Yes, she was a single woman about to have a baby, but there were hundreds of women living in the city under the same or worse circumstances. This secret wish to pay her rent or to fill her fridge with groceries was ridiculous.

Proof, really, that he was allowing himself to get emotionally involved. Something both Brock and Joe had warned him against.

He did his best to fight off the need to comfort her. "Sit down," he suggested. "I should look at those blisters on your feet again."

"I can do it. My stomach isn't that big that I can't reach my toes." She shrugged out of her coat and sat. "I'm so thankful for these running shoes."

He sat in the chair perpendicular to the sofa, keeping distance between them. "Are you hungry? I can order room service."

She nodded. "I should eat something. But nothing spicy," she hastily added. "I had Mexican last week and suffered heartburn all night afterward."

"I don't think Mexican is on the menu." He rose and grabbed the menu. "There isn't a lot to choose from."

"It's fine." She eyed the brief list of options. "The chicken ranch wrap sounds good. Thank you."

He placed an order for a cheeseburger and her chicken wrap. A text came in from Brock. *Shell casings match those found at the previous scenes.*

He texted back. *Anything else?*

Brown SUV abandoned five blocks from the church. Techs are sweeping it now.

He hoped and prayed there would be trace DNA found in the SUV. *Good. We're at City Central with Rhy's SUV.*

Brock responded with the okay sign.

"News?" Harper asked.

He filled her in on the evidence that was found so far. She sighed and shook her head. "That all sounds good, but we're really no closer to finding this guy."

"I know. But every mistake he makes will add up. Once we grab him, we'll have plenty of evidence to keep him in jail for a long time."

"Unless he has a lot of money, like Neil Otterson," she murmured.

"That's true." The legal system wasn't always fair. Those with money rarely did jail time while awaiting trial, while those without money often did. It was one argument in favor of setting low bail amounts. Yet as a cop, it galled him to know that criminals could hurt others, then be out on the street within twenty-four hours to continue breaking the law.

"I don't understand why they tried to kidnap me at first but now have resorted to shooting at me."

That dichotomy had been bugging him too. "I can't understand why the goal is to kill you either. You're not a threat to Tommy Grotto."

"I'm not a threat to anyone," she corrected. "Not Jake, not Grotto or any of his buddies."

A rap on their door had him jumping to his feet. He didn't open the door until he verified the hotel staff member was on the other side. Ironically, it was the same guy who'd served their suite last month while protecting Elly. By the way the guy's eyes widened, Steele assumed the staff member remembered him too.

"Thanks." He took the tray, then passed him a tip.

The guy backed out of the room without saying anything more.

He gestured for Harper to join him at the table. "Let's eat."

She rose and crossed the room to sit beside him. This was exactly the kind of thing that made it difficult to keep her at a distance. There was way too much togetherness.

He should have asked Brock or Joe to come to the hotel too. Better yet, he should let one of them stay here with Harper while he returned to the crime scene.

He mentally grimaced. Yeah, no matter how much he lectured himself, he knew he wouldn't make that call.

"I'd like to say grace." Harper's soft voice was not helping.

He cleared his throat. "Sure." When she held out her hand, he took it. How could he not?

"Dear Lord Jesus, thank You for keeping us all safe in Your loving arms today. We ask that You please continue to guide Steele, Brock, Joe, and the others to the truth, while keeping them safe under Your shield of protection. Amen."

"Amen." Her sweet words were humbling. And somehow, he felt stronger with the thought of God watching over them. Guiding them. Protecting them.

If he were honest, it was the only explanation as to how they'd managed to evade these gunmen over and over again.

Was this how Rhy and Joe felt about their faith? He didn't know and wasn't about to ask. Most men he knew kept that sort of thing private.

But maybe that was the wrong approach. What did he know?

When Harper released his hand, he glanced at her to find she was watching him. Her sweet smile stole his breath. "Thanks for praying with me."

"Anytime." Really? What was wrong with him? He cut his cheeseburger in half and took a big bite to keep from making other rash promises.

Promises he likely couldn't keep.

They ate in silence for a moment. Steele tried to think of a neutral topic of conversation but came up empty.

"I don't like the way someone got into my apartment," Harper said with a frown. "Is it really that easy?"

"It can be." He hadn't studied the inside of her building closely. "I would have to see it myself to know for sure."

She hesitated, then asked, "I don't want to be a bother, but would you be willing to change my door locks once this is over?"

"Yes, absolutely." He told himself he would make the same offer to any single mother. This wasn't a promise to support her. Just a helping hand to a woman in need. "It's not a bother. You have your baby to think about."

"Yes, and that's what worries me."

He took another bite of his burger. The early darkness outside made it seem later than it was. Maybe she'd get some rest once they'd finished their meal.

"Oh!" Harper's exclamation startled him. She dropped her hands to her belly.

"What is it? Something wrong? More cramps? Contractions?" He couldn't hide his panic.

"No, she's just really active." She reached over to grab his hand and placed it on her swollen belly. Beneath his fingers, he could feel the baby moving.

"That was a kick!" He had never felt anything like it. "She actually kicked me."

"She does that a lot." Harper smiled, still pressing her hand over his. "It's amazing, isn't it?"

You're amazing. He almost said the words out loud. And it took every ounce of willpower he possessed not to draw her into his arms and kiss her.

CHAPTER SEVEN

Harper's breath caught in her throat, her blood surging through her veins. Sharing this intimate moment of her baby kicking with Steele was incredible. His intense blue gaze bored into hers, and she thought he was about to kiss her.

But then he slid his hand from beneath hers and abruptly stood. He looked everywhere but at her. "I—ah, need to make a few calls."

"Okay." Missing the warmth of his hand on her belly, she turned and stacked their dinner dishes on the tray, struggling to maintain an impassive expression. These stolen moments were amazing, but they weren't real. She knew Steele was only sticking close to protect her.

He was a genuinely nice guy. So different from Jake. Although her ex-husband had been nice in the beginning too.

Would Steele change over time? She didn't think so, but her track record with men wasn't great. Even now she was clearly having trouble distinguishing between fantasy and reality.

Her reality was heading back to work as soon as possible, then giving birth to her child. A man and a relationship weren't in her immediate future. She didn't trust a man enough to open herself up to being hurt. Although if she ever did decide to try again, it would be with a man like Steele. Someone handsome, honorable, kind, and strong, while being gentle at the same time.

Maybe someday . . .

But not now. She finished stacking the dishes and rose to carry the tray to the door. Steele immediately jumped forward. "I'll take that."

"It's not heavy." Her protest fell on deaf ears.

Steele took a moment to eye the hallway through the peephole and then opened the door to set the tray of dishes on the floor. Then he closed the door and shot the deadbolt home. His phone pinged, and he frowned as he reached for it. After glancing at the screen, he said, "This is Perkins."

It took her a moment to place the name. Oh yes, Perkins and Banner were the two ATF agents. Was that one of the calls he'd made? "Does he have good news? Is the shooter in custody?"

"Not exactly." His frown deepened. He pressed on the screen, then lifted the phone to his ear. "What's going on, Perkins? Why the sudden desire to interview Ms. Crane?"

Interview her? Her stomach knotted, and she took several deep breaths to remain calm. She hadn't done anything wrong. There was no reason to be nervous about an interview with the ATF.

A flash of annoyance hit hard. She had told Steele and Brock everything she knew during their first interview, right after she'd almost been kidnapped. Why did she have to repeat herself? What was the point?

Shouldn't they be spending their time on more important things? Like searching for Tommy Grotto and his shooters?

"Yeah, okay. If you insist. We can do that tomorrow morning." There was another pause before Steele said, "Nine works. See you then."

"Why do they want to interview me?"

He looked frustrated, too, but shrugged. "I don't know. To be fair, they didn't get a chance to talk to you since this started."

"I don't know anything!" She tried to dial back her anger. "It's a stupid waste of time. They should be looking for Tommy Grotto and his buddies."

"They are." He smiled reassuringly. "This is mostly a formality. A task that needs to be done, nothing more. Especially now that Ellis Starkey has been murdered."

"It's still stupid." She sighed and shook her head. "Whatever. I hate knowing Ellis was killed. I don't think he deserved to be. Yet interviewing me isn't going to help them find the person responsible. I honestly wish it would. I wish I knew something that would put a stop to all of this." She stared down at her abdomen for a long moment. "I would give anything to go back to my boring life."

"I know. I hate that you're going through this." Steele stood awkwardly in the center of the suite. "You should get some rest. Sounds like it may be a long day tomorrow."

"Yes." She was exhausted. Emotionally more so than physically. Being on high alert for danger was wearing her down. She lifted her head to meet Steele's gaze. "We're really safe here?"

"Yes. No more trackers, remember?" He smiled. "We have Rhy's SUV to use for the foreseeable future. Brock and Joe are heading home after they finish up processing the crime scene."

"Okay." She stood and moved toward the closest bedroom. All she had were the clothes on her back, borrowed ones at that. Still, she felt blessed to be alive. "Good night."

"Good night." Steele's low, husky voice seemed to follow her into the room. Now she was being even more ridiculous.

After washing up in the bathroom, she bent to remove her running shoes and socks. Her blisters were still red and sore, but they looked better. She decided to leave the bandages off for the night. She could reapply the antibiotic ointment in the morning.

Her physical fatigue lulled her to sleep. But she awoke a few hours later, her heart pounding with fear. Gunshots? Had they been found?

She listened intently, then forced herself to relax. It was a dream. They were safe. If there had been gunfire, Steele would have barged in to get her.

Unless he was dead?

With the baby pressing on her bladder, she had to get up anyway. After a quick trip to the bathroom, she padded to the door and listened. Hearing nothing, she opened the door a crack and peered through.

It took a moment for her eyes to adjust. Movement on the sofa drew her attention. When a head popped up, she realized Steele was stretched out there.

"What's wrong?" His voice was groggy with sleep. "Are you okay?"

"Yes, sorry. Just checking." It sounded lame, so she added, "This is my usual midnight bathroom break."

"Did you have a nightmare?" His astute question caught her off guard.

"I thought I heard gunfire." She was glad the darkness

hid her flush of embarrassment. "It was only my imagination."

"I should have warned you about having flashbacks." Steele looked and sounded more awake now, as he swung into a sitting position on the sofa. "You've been through a traumatic experience."

"I know." It was nice of him to try to make her feel better. She doubted he suffered nightmares after hearing gunfire. "Sorry to have bothered you."

"You didn't. I was only dozing." He stood and moved toward her. Glancing down at her bare feet, he frowned. "I should take care of them for you."

"No need. Tomorrow morning I'll take a shower and put more ointment on." The memory of how tenderly he'd cared for her injuries was front and center in her mind. "I'm fine."

"Okay." He stood there as if searching for something more to say.

She stepped forward and lifted up onto her tiptoes to kiss his cheek. "You're a nice guy, Steele. Good night."

"Ah, good night." He stood still, as if rooted in place. "Sweet dreams."

She nodded, ducked into her room, and closed her door. She leaned against it, her knees feeling weak. For a moment, she'd thought he might pull her close, but he didn't. Just like earlier, she was letting her imagination run wild.

Pregnancy hormones, she reminded herself. Who knew how potent they could be?

After a moment, she pushed away from the door and crawled back into bed.

Steele had chosen to sleep on the sofa despite the suite having two bedrooms to be in a better position to protect her. And he'd awoken at the slightest noise she'd made opening her bedroom door.

No one had ever cared about her as much as he did. Well, except for her parents, but they were gone. Tears of gratitude mixed with despair over wanting what she could never have pricked her eyes as she willed herself to return to sleep.

THE FAINT LIGHT of dawn was just on the horizon when Steele awoke. He hadn't slept well, partially because the sofa was too short to be comfortable and partially because of the way Harper had kissed his cheek.

There was something seriously wrong with him that he had trouble falling back to sleep because all he could think about was kissing Harper. Not on the cheek, and not in a brotherly fashion.

Why did his memories of Monique seem so blurry? Two years had passed, but he'd had no intention of moving on. Especially not with a pregnant woman.

He really needed to get a grip. Being here with Harper was messing with his determination to remain single. After losing Monique, he'd lost interest in settling down, but now it seemed he couldn't imagine moving on with his old life. One that didn't include Harper.

And her baby? He gave himself a mental shake. She was a package deal. An adorable package deal, but he wasn't ready for that level of commitment.

Was he?

Nope. He stood and headed to the small coffee maker. A good jolt of caffeine should help keep him focused on the important issues facing them.

Not his personal life.

Hearing sounds of movement from Harper's room reminded him of her blisters. He crossed over and lightly rapped on her door. "Harper? I'll help you bandage your feet when you're ready."

"Okay." Her voice sounded muffled as if she might be in the bathroom.

He poured himself a cup of coffee, then guiltily remembered she could only drink decaf. Rummaging in the small basket beside the pot, he found a package of decaf. He'd make that as soon as he'd finished the real stuff.

While he waited, he booted up the computer and began searching on Starkey, Waylon Brooks, and Tommy Grotto. They'd tried routine searches before but had come up empty. Yet there was always the possibility that something new might pop up, especially on social media. He'd heard of criminals doing illegal business through social media sites. It sounded crazy, yet they hadn't gotten caught right away.

The internet was full of information. The only problem was that he needed to sort through all the junk and fake news to get to the real intel.

Harper stepped out of her room a few minutes later. She held her shoes and socks in one hand and the antibiotic ointment in the other. "My blisters look much better this morning."

"Glad to hear it." Maybe his fear of her wounds becoming infected was irrational, but he didn't want to take any chances. "Let me see."

She dropped onto the sofa. He knelt beside her, taking a moment to examine her toes. The reddened areas were still there, but they weren't weeping the way they had been. He nodded in satisfaction. "They do look much better. Do they hurt?"

"Not nearly as much as before."

"Good. I think we should put more ointment on, though. Just to be on the safe side."

"Okay. I took a bath but didn't shower since I don't have anything to use on my hair." She touched the long blond strands self-consciously. "I would love to pick up a hairbrush and some other toiletries to replace those we left behind at the American Lodge."

"You're beautiful, and we might be able to stop on the way home from the precinct." He wasn't lying to make her feel better. He took the tube of ointment from her hand and turned his attention back to her feet.

"Jesus washed the feet of his apostles," she said in a low voice, "to show how much he cared for them. And to show how he wasn't any better than they were, despite being sent by God."

"Really?" He glanced at her in surprise. "I hate to say it, but I don't know much about the Bible."

"Maybe someday you'll have time to learn." He was glad she wasn't being pushy about it. He'd never been interested enough to read the Bible, but the image of Jesus washing the feet of his apostles stuck with him.

When he finished with the ointment, he helped her with the socks and shoes. Then he stood and shoved his hands into his pockets to keep from reaching for her. "Ah, I forgot about the decaf, so I'll have to make a new pot."

"It's fine." She waved toward the small kitchenette. "I can heat up water in the microwave for herbal tea. No need for you to sacrifice caffeine for my sake."

"Okay." This constant awareness of her made him feel awkward. "Just let me know when you want to order breakfast."

She crossed to the kitchenette to make her herbal tea.

Glancing at the computer, she asked, "Are you checking emails?"

"No, just trying to find information on our perps." He sipped his coffee, waiting for her to finish.

"Like on social media?" She wrinkled her nose. "That seems silly. It's not like a criminal is going to post stuff on there for everyone to see."

"No, but you'd be surprised at how many people with criminal records are actually friends with other criminals." He shrugged. "But so far I haven't found anything useful, so you're probably right about it being a waste of time."

"I'm not the expert. You are." She took the seat next to him. The space was small enough that their knees brushed. "I gave up social media. I found myself comparing my situation to others and decided it was a silly way to spend my time."

"I'm not on there, except for a dummy page." He shrugged. "Most cops avoid that stuff. Rhy always said that cops were enough of a target without making it easy for people to find us."

"True. I hadn't thought of it that way." She frowned. "I should have thanked you for getting me away from the American Lodge. I'm so glad Brock and Joe weren't injured."

"They're fine. And you don't need to thank us." He didn't want or need her gratitude. "It's our fault for not doing a better job of keeping you safe."

She sipped her tea, then leaned forward to grab the menu. "I can't believe I'm hungry."

"Eating for two, remember?" He finished his first cup of coffee while she decided on breakfast. Then he placed their order.

"You're sure this interview is necessary?" she asked when he'd finished.

"The ATF thinks so." He didn't want to admit that he wasn't happy about their request. It's a risk they shouldn't have to take. He trusted the ATF agents, but not enough to have them come meet at the hotel. In his opinion, their location was a need to know, and they didn't need to know. "We'll leave here around eight thirty. I'll take the long way to the precinct."

"Sounds good." She glanced around the suite. "This is a really nice place. I hope the police department is reimbursing you."

He had no idea if Rhy or Assistant Chief Michaels would ultimately get the department to cover the cost, but she didn't need to worry about that. "It's fine. Not as expensive as some places."

"What about the damage to the American Lodge?"

"We'll take care of that too." He reached over to pat her hand. "Harper, just concentrate on relaxing for the sake of the baby, okay? This other stuff isn't important."

"Okay, I'll try."

Thankfully, their breakfast arrived in record time. He jumped up, dug out some cash for a tip, and set the tray on the table. As irritated as he was about the need for the ATF to interview Harper, spending the day with her alone was driving him nuts.

Harper had closed and moved the computer to make room. The scent of bacon and eggs made his mouth water. He lifted both domes, setting them aside.

This time he was prepared for Harper to say grace. "Dear Lord Jesus, we are so blessed by this food You've provided to us. We ask that You please continue to keep everyone on the tactical team safe in Your care. Amen."

"Amen. Thanks for keeping us in your prayers." He glanced at her before reaching for his fork. "It's much appreciated."

"Always," she said lightly. "I respect the work you do very much."

Thirty minutes later, they were out in Rhy's SUV. Harper still wore his coat, but she had to leave it open as it didn't fit over her stomach. Thankfully, the area outside the side door of the hotel was empty. Once Harper was seated, he ran around to take the wheel.

The trip took longer than he'd expected because traffic was a bear. An accident on one side of the interstate had brought them to a standstill. *Stupid gawkers*, he thought, feeling impatient.

They managed to get to the precinct with about ten minutes to spare. Steele had no doubt the ATF agents were already in the conference room waiting. Yet he took the added precaution of driving around back and parking Rhy's SUV near the exit.

"To think I've never been inside a police station until I became a victim of a crime." She shook her head as Steele escorted her inside. "There are times I can barely remember what my life was like before all of this."

"Things will get back to normal soon," he assured her.

"I hope so." She stood to the side as he closed the door, then he led the way through the cubicles.

Flynn Ryerson came walking toward him. "Hey, Steele. I heard you guys are working some hot leads on the warehouse case."

"I'm not sure they're hot," he responded in a wry tone. "Flynn, this is Harper Crane. Harper, Flynn is another member on the tactical team."

"You're not in uniform," she said. "Do you have the day off?"

"I'm on sick leave until my arm heals up." He made a fist and bent his elbow up and down. "It's getting there."

"What happened?" For some reason, the concern in Harper's gaze made him want to stand between her and Flynn.

"Bullet grazed my arm during the warehouse shooting." Flynn glanced at Steele. "Steve Banner saved my life."

"He did?" That was news to Steele.

"Yeah. He shot the guy who fired at me before he could get off a second round." Flynn massaged his bicep. "I'm hoping to be cleared to return to duty next week."

"Take all the time you need." Steele grinned. "We'll have this case wrapped up by then no problem."

"You should," Flynn shot back. Then he smiled again at Harper. "Nice to meet you, Harper. Later, Steele."

Flynn left through the same side door they'd entered. He told himself that Flynn was just being his usual easygoing self. Not flirting with Harper.

"Are we using the same interview room as last time?" Harper glanced around. "I don't remember where it is."

"This way." He escorted her to the interview room. As predicted, both Steve Banner and Bryon Perkins were already there waiting.

"Ms. Crane." Banner stood and offered his hand. "I'm Agent Steve Banner. This is my partner, Bryon Perkins."

Perkins shook her hand too.

"I guess you both know who I am," she murmured, taking the chair directly across from them.

"Yes, ma'am," Bryon said.

"Please call me Harper." She folded her hands on the table, but Steele had noticed her fingers were trembling. "I want to help in any way I can. I'm afraid that I don't know anything, though." She glanced at him, then added, "Officer Delaney and Officer Greer questioned me after I was almost kidnapped."

"We heard." Banner looked annoyed for a moment, but then he smiled. "We appreciate you taking the time to speak with us too."

Harper nodded, then waited for them to move on.

"Ms—er, Harper, can you tell us when you last saw Ellis Starkey?" Bryon Perkins asked.

"It was probably a week or two before I left my husband." She stared down at her hands for a moment. "I haven't seen Jake in over seven months. Since the night . . ." Her voice trailed off, and a flush darkened her cheeks.

Banner seemed to take pity on her. "So roughly seven and a half months ago was the last time you saw Ellis Starkey? Would that be correct?"

"Yes. As far as I remember." She frowned. "Ellis and Jake were business partners. Legitimate business, or so I thought. Anyway, Ellis stopped by on occasion, so it wasn't really like a visit with him would stick out in my mind, you know?"

"Sure, that makes sense," Banner said. "How long did you know him?"

"Two and a half years." She answered without hesitation. "I wouldn't say we were close or anything, but he was Jake's best friend and stood up at our wedding. He came across as a nice guy. That's why I was so shocked to learn about their illegal business dealings."

"You mean the buying and selling of guns," Perkins pressed.

"Yes. That's what I was told." She lifted her chin and looked directly at Bryon. "I never saw any guns for myself."

"You didn't go to the warehouses at all?" Doubt tinged Bryon's tone.

"Never. Why would I?" She shrugged. "I kept busy with my full-time job."

"Yes, working for Gibson and Roberts, right?" Steve asked.

"That's right." She didn't expound on that, and Steele was proud of her for maintaining her cool professionalism. He knew the two ATF agents were just doing their job, but he resented the implication she was hiding something from them.

"I still find it hard to believe you never went to the warehouses," Bryon said. "Unless, of course, you knew what your ex-husband was doing."

"I didn't." Her voice was calm, but Steele caught the flash of anger in her green eyes. She leaned forward. "I would never condone selling guns. I work for an attorney. Do you really think I'd allow my ex-husband to drag me down with him?"

"A criminal defense attorney," Bryon pointed out. "Seems like your boss deals with criminals all the time."

"Alleged criminals." Her chin tipped higher. "Innocent until proven guilty in a court of law, right?"

Neither ATF agent said anything for a long moment. Harper didn't speak either. She sat calmly, waiting for their next question.

Finally, Steve asked, "Do you know where we can find Tommy Grotto? Or Waylon Brooks?"

"No. If I did, I would tell you since it's highly likely one or both of them have tried to shoot me." She shook her head and sighed. "Really, why won't you believe me? Do you honestly think I'd risk the life of my baby by holding back the truth? Because I can tell you I would never do that.

Never."

"Look, guys, she's told you what she knows." Steele stepped forward, determined to put an end to this.

"This interview isn't over until we say it is," Perkins snapped.

Steve Banner was obviously playing the role of good cop. "Harper, we have one more question." He opened an envelope and slid a photograph across the table. "Can you tell me who this is?"

Steele clenched his jaw when he saw the picture of Harper chatting with a man while standing on a sidewalk. The man she was talking to was none other than Kenny Dillon, a.k.a. Dillweed.

One of the three men who were killed during the shoot-out at her ex-husband's warehouse.

CHAPTER EIGHT

Harper stared at the glossy photograph the ATF agent slid across the table. It was eerie to see her standing there talking to a man when she had no idea anyone was close enough to take a picture of her.

Just how long had they been following her?

"Harper?" Steele prodded.

She glanced at him, shocked to see wary suspicion simmering in his eyes. She didn't understand the significance of this picture. "This is Glenn Vice. He attends my church sometimes."

"Your church?" The scathing doubt in Perkins's tone was like nails on a chalkboard. "You really expect us to believe that?"

She abruptly pushed the photograph back across the table toward him. "Yes. We are standing on the sidewalk outside the church. And if you were there taking this picture, you already know that."

"How well do you know Glenn Vice?" Steele asked.

It hurt to know he was grilling her like a suspect. Like spending five minutes chatting with a fellow church member was wrong. She didn't look at Steele, keeping her gaze focused on the two ATF agents across from her. "I don't know him very well at all. We ended up sitting in the same pew, and he introduced himself. I returned the favor. We chatted for a few minutes after services, and that was the end of it."

"He didn't ask you to go out with him? Dinner or a movie?" Steve Banner asked.

"No." Then she amended her statement. "Sort of. He mentioned his favorite restaurant, a steak place I'd never heard of. I told him to enjoy and turned away. Maybe he intended to ask me out, but it didn't happen." She crossed her arms over her chest. "What does Glenn Vice have to do with anything?"

"He's dead," Bryon Perkins said bluntly. "Killed in the shooting at your ex-husband's warehouse two weeks ago."

That was a surprise. "You're saying he worked for Jake?"

"His name isn't Glenn Vice," Steele said. "His real name is Kenny Dillon, a.k.a. Dillweed."

The tiny hairs on the back of her neck rose in alarm. Glenn was Kenny? He'd worked for her ex? And had tried to get close to her by attending the same church she did? "I had no idea."

"How often did you see Dillweed at church?" Perkins asked.

She clenched her jaw, holding back a sharp retort. "I saw the man I knew as Glenn Vice about three times. He wasn't always at services. And to be honest, I wasn't always able to attend either."

"I thought that was part of your routine?" Steele said.

It took all her willpower to remain calm. "Yes, except for the early days in my pregnancy when I suffered morning sickness. And there was the time I came down with a bad cold. Then there was that snowstorm too." She thought back to the times she'd stayed home on a Sunday. "On a rare occasion, Trent Gibson would ask me to do some work from home on the weekend. If I didn't get to it on Saturday, I'd get caught up on Sunday." Now she turned in her seat. "Do you want me to ask my boss for evidence of each time I worked from home?"

Steele shook his head, but his expression remained serious. "That's not necessary. We're just trying to understand the connection between you and Kenny Dillon."

"There is only a vague connection between me and Glenn Vice." She didn't care if she sounded obstinate. There was nothing she could do to force them to believe her. "I have no idea why he pretended to be someone else. Or why he attended church services."

"To get close to you, of course," Perkins said.

She stared at Perkins and decided she didn't like him. He was being a jerk for no good reason. "Is that all? Or do you have other questions for me?"

"We'd like to search your apartment." Steve Banner offered a sympathetic smile. "With your permission of course."

"Go ahead." Her response was immediate. "You won't find anything."

"Keep in mind, Brock and I were there when someone tried to kidnap Harper," Steele said, seeming to come to her defense for the first time since this interview started. "She also had a tracking device on her car, her shoe, and maybe even in her purse. It's not a stretch to believe they planted someone at the church to get close to her."

"Okay, but why go to all that trouble?" Perkins asked. "What's the motive behind tracking her and trying to kill her?" His gaze cut to her. "Unless she's involved, and they're afraid she'll talk to save herself."

"If she was involved, she'd already be dead," Steele said. "You know that as well as I do."

"Maybe." Perkins shrugged. "I'm not ready to concede to anything yet."

She'd had enough of this. "I'd like to be there when you search my apartment. I wouldn't mind getting some personal items too. Like toiletries."

The two ATF agents exchanged a long look. Finally, Banner nodded. "That's fine. But you can't take anything until after we're finished with the search."

"I understand." She rose to her feet, praying for strength. She refused to fall apart in front of these guys. She didn't really care what they thought about her.

But she did care about Steele's opinion. Far more than she should.

"We'll meet you at the apartment," Steele said. He rested his hand in the small of her back. It was ridiculous to be comforted by the gesture.

She left the room, leaving the guys to follow. She spied a bathroom and, desperate for a few minutes alone, quickly veered toward it.

Steele let her go, no doubt taking the time to discuss the interview with the ATF. Alone in the restroom, she leaned against the wall and buried her face in her hands. Discovering Jake was a criminal wasn't as humiliating as that interview was. Especially when they'd shown her the photograph they'd taken without her knowledge.

How could they believe she was involved? It didn't make any sense. It wasn't like she was spending a bunch of money or hiding large sums of cash. She lived paycheck to paycheck; there was a laughable amount of money in her checking account.

Her pathetic financial situation helped calm her nerves. Okay, they'd caught her talking to one of Jake's employees. Big deal. It didn't mean anything. As far as she could remember, that was the only time she'd spoken to Glenn, or Dillweed, or whoever he was.

Once they'd finished searching her apartment, she'd be exonerated. Of course, the fact that she'd been the victim of an attempted kidnapping and the target of gunfire should have already done that.

A harsh laugh escaped her tight throat. She drew a deep breath and let it out slowly, reminding herself for the millionth time that stress wasn't good for the baby.

After using the facilities and washing her face and hands, she felt better. When she emerged from the restroom, Steele straightened, his gaze searching hers. "Are you okay?"

"Peachy." She pasted a smile onto her features. "Let's go. I want to be there when they search."

"Harper . . ."

"No." She cut him off. "I don't want to talk about it. It's clear they suspect me of being involved in Jake's business. I've already told you, and them, that I'm not. Believe what you want."

"I believe you're innocent," Steele said in a low voice.

"Really?" She scoffed. "That's now how it came across to me."

"Harper, listen." He caught her hand. "I admit I was caught off guard seeing that photograph of you talking to Dillweed. But I know you're not involved in this. I know you're innocent."

She wanted so badly to believe him. To have him

believe in her. But it wasn't easy. Especially after that grueling interview. "I am innocent."

"I know." He searched her gaze for a moment, then surprised her by bringing her hand up to kiss it. "I'm not going anywhere. I'll continue to protect you until we get to the bottom of this mess."

The icy wall she'd built around her heart melted just a bit. "Thank you." She rested her free hand on her belly. "I appreciate that."

He stepped closer, as if to pull her into his arms, but a voice called out, "Delaney?"

"What's up, Brock?" He turned to face his colleague.

"I heard about the search." Brock actually looked concerned for her welfare. "Do you want company?"

"No thanks, we have Rhy's SUV." Steele shrugged. "They're just covering all bases."

"Yeah." Brock's expression still looked troubled. "If you're okay, then I'll head back to the American Lodge. I'd like to search the place again in the daylight. Make sure we didn't miss anything."

"Sounds good," Steele agreed. "Keep me updated on your progress."

"Will do." Brock nodded at her, then headed for the side door.

"Wait up," Steele called. "Let's cover Harper as we leave."

Being in a police station should be safe enough, but she didn't protest as the two men protected her until she was situated in the passenger seat of Rhy's SUV. Steele said something briefly to Brock, then slid in behind the wheel.

The ride to her apartment was unusually silent. She looked out the window, searching for the brown SUV, until she remembered it had been found abandoned not far from the American Lodge.

Steele hadn't mentioned recovering evidence from the vehicle. Maybe it was too soon to expect that. This wasn't TV. DNA and other testing took time.

Time she might not have.

The sobering thought hit hard. She pushed the fear away, focusing on deep breathing and other relaxation techniques. Maybe there wasn't anything she could do to change the minds of the ATF agents about her innocence, but she could do a better job of caring for her baby.

When Steele drove up to the front of her brick apartment building, she was struck by how run-down it looked. The peeling paint and occasional missing brick hadn't bothered her before. She'd been grateful to find a place she could afford.

Yet she did her best to ignore the shabby structure. When Steele shifted the gear shift into park, she reached for the door handle.

"Wait for me," he said. "I'll cover you."

She could see there were two men standing just inside the front door. Steele came around, opened her door, and covered her as she slid out. Then he scanned the area as they headed up the sidewalk.

Steve Banner opened the door for her. She managed a smile. "Thank you."

Perkins headed up the stairs to the second floor first, leaving her and the others to follow. She'd left her purse at Steele's house, so she didn't have a key. But somehow, Perkins had one and unlocked the door.

"Your manager," he said by way of explanation as he crossed the threshold.

She vaguely wondered if this was how Tommy Grotto's

men had gotten inside to plant the tracking devices. Security obviously wasn't a high priority.

"Please stay out of the way," Banner said.

"She needs to sit in a chair," Steele said. He stepped into the kitchen, grabbed one, and brought it over to the small entryway near the cheap table she'd used to display the blue vase Ellis had given her. The plastic flowers she'd placed in the vase drooped to one side.

She sat, mostly because her knees felt weak. She'd never expected to be in a situation like this.

Watching the ATF agents go through her cupboards and drawers made her feel sick to her stomach. They searched methodically, obviously used to it. They flipped her sofa cushions on the floor, rifled through the small stack of library books on her end table, then went as far as to lift the sofa up on one end to look underneath.

When they moved into her bedroom, she closed her eyes, not wanting to imagine them going through her personal things. Her underwear, her bathroom toiletries. Nothing would be off limits.

"Delaney?" Steve Banner called. "You're going to want to see this."

See what? She shot to her feet, following Steele into her bedroom. Her cheeks flushed as she saw her underwear tossed to the floor in a haphazard pile.

Her blood ran cold when she saw the gun sitting beside her lacy bra. No, it couldn't be. She didn't own a gun. Had never even touched one.

Yet as Perkins's accusing gaze locked on hers, she knew protesting would be useless. Whoever had come into her apartment to place those tracking devices had also planted this gun.

She swallowed hard, wondering if she was destined to have her baby in prison.

———————

"IT'S A SIG SAUER," Banner said, as if he couldn't figure that out for himself.

Steele scowled. "Using her underwear drawer is predictable, don't you think? Grotto's men could have stashed it here when they planted those trackers."

"Maybe," Banner agreed. "Then again, maybe not."

He didn't for one second believe that weapon was Harper's. But he was careful to maintain a professional demeanor in front of the ATF agents. "I'm only pointing out the obvious, exactly the way a good defense attorney would."

Perkins carefully placed the weapon in an evidence bag. "That theory won't fly if her prints are found on the gun."

Her prints could be planted there, too, but he held back from stating the obvious. The SIG Sauer was used by plenty of military and law enforcement personnel. And it was also the likely weapon used in these recent shootings. Yet if a woman like Harper wanted a gun for self-defense, she'd likely pick something smaller.

"We'll get this tested ASAP," Banner said.

"Go ahead. It's not my gun." Harper turned and left the room. He wanted to follow but forced himself to stand there while the ATF agents finished searching the room.

When they didn't find anything else, he eyed them warily. "You know that gun was planted."

"We don't know that," Perkins shot back.

"I assume you've gone over Harper's financial records." He kept his voice even, even though he wanted nothing more than to plant his fist in Perkins's face. "Find anything suspicious there?"

"No, but she could have a secret account we don't know about." Perkins seemed intent on believing the worst. "Maybe she convinced Dillweed to hide money for her."

"Yeah, and how does that work now that he's dead?" When he realized he'd curled his fingers into fists, he forced himself to relax. "I'm anxious to see what the lab will come up with when they test the weapon."

"Even if it's clean, it could be one of Grotto's guns," Banner said.

Yeah, that was likely true. Of course, Grotto would have one of his men stash a hot gun in Harper's apartment.

But again, the motive for this was fuzzy. If Grotto and his men were truly trying to set her up to take the fall, why bother shooting at her? Or trying to kidnap her? They could have easily used an anonymous tip to get them to this point. The same way a tip had led to her ex-husband's arrest.

It didn't make any sense.

"Are you planning to arrest her?" Steele forced himself to sound matter of fact.

"No," Banner said. Perkins simply scowled. "As you pointed out, there are too many unanswered questions here." Banner shrugged. "We'll wait for ballistics and finger-print testing to be completed."

Small comfort, but he nodded. "Then I'm going to take her someplace safe."

"Hold on, Delaney," Perkins protested. "Who died and made you the woman's protector?"

"I picked the short straw." That wasn't true, but he was tired of Perkins's attitude. "Why does it matter who protects her? She's been targeted by gunfire nonstop over the past few days. It's only by God's grace that she's still alive."

Perkins shrugged. "Seems Grotto is worried she's going to spill the beans."

"A valid point if she had any information to give." He shifted to look at Banner. "Think about this logically. She's pregnant. Don't you think she'd drop the dime on these guys in a heartbeat to protect her baby?"

"Yeah, I do," Banner admitted.

"Maybe" was all Perkins would say. "Or this is all an elaborate ruse to send us off track."

He wasn't sure what Perkins's problem was, and he didn't care. The guy was being obstinate about his theory that Harper was holding back key information. The ATF guys hadn't spent the last two days with her the way he had.

Swallowing a sigh, he turned and headed back to the living area. He found Harper sitting on the chair near the door, her head bowed and her hands clasped on her rounded belly. It took him a moment to realize she was praying.

He stood for a moment, watching and waiting for her to finish. When she lifted her head, he saw the flash of pure anguish in her eyes.

His heart squeezed in his chest. The setup was obvious to him, but he couldn't prevent the ATF agents from considering all angles.

"Am I going to have my baby in jail?" Her question made him wince.

"No." He crossed over to kneel beside her.

"Don't patronize me," she warned. "I deserve honesty."

She did. "You're not under arrest, Harper. But I don't control the ATF either. They're sending the weapon for testing. Those results will determine their next steps."

She didn't say anything right away. "Am I free to gather some of my personal items? Toiletries and such?"

"I'll ask." He hesitated, then said, "Harper, you might want to call your boss, Trent Gibson. Do you think he'll represent you pro bono?"

"Are you seriously asking me that?" Her temper flared, and she shot to her feet, shoving him out of her way. "I'm getting my things."

"Wait." He caught her hand, then let go when she shot him a narrow look. "Harper, listen to me. You wanted honesty. I'm giving it to you. I don't want you to talk to the ATF agents any more without your lawyer present. Do you understand?"

"What about you? Shouldn't I have my lawyer present when we're talking?"

It was a good point. "The illegal gun trafficking falls into the jurisdiction of the ATF. And since I've been with you the past few days, they'd have to recuse me from the case anyway. I would end up being a witness in your defense."

"You can leave anytime." She held his gaze. "Pawn me off on someone else if you'd like."

"I'm not interested in leaving you, Harper." That was true on many levels, he realized grimly. Not that this was the time or place to discuss it. "Get your personal things together and we'll hit the road."

She turned away and went back to her room. He followed, watching from the doorway. Perkins and Banner stepped back, giving her space.

She pulled a small backpack from her closet and turned to her dresser. Revulsion crossed her features as she bent to replace the underwear the ATF agents had tossed onto the floor. She stuffed a few items into her bag, then left the bedroom to grab a few items from the bathroom. Then in the kitchen, she tossed in another container of prenatal vitamins.

Less than five minutes later, she was back at the chair by the doorway. "I'm ready."

His heart ached for her. The stoic expression on his face didn't fool him. She was devastated by this. And he didn't blame her for being upset.

For a split second, he wondered if Perkins had planted the gun there. Then he quickly shoved that thought aside. No, that was too obvious. If Perkins had planted a gun, he wouldn't want to be the cop that found it.

Besides, he didn't believe the ATF agents were involved in the gunrunning operation. They'd been active participants in the shoot-out at the warehouse, same as their tactical team. Banner had saved Flynn's life when he was wounded.

Buying into the planted gun was lazy investigating. And that irked him. He made a mental note to check in with Rhy when they were back at the City Central Hotel. Rhy would need to brief Assistant Chief Michaels on this latest twist in the case.

And he really needed to convince Harper to talk to her boss. At the very least to put Trent Gibson on notice that she might need his legal services.

"I'm ready to go," Harper repeated.

"Okay." He reached for the bag, but she didn't hand it over. "I'll carry that for you."

"I have it." She wouldn't look him directly in the eye. "Just get me out of here, okay? I don't feel well."

He didn't think she was referring to her pregnancy. He nodded and opened the apartment door for her. After checking the hallway, he stepped out. "Stay behind me."

She didn't answer, but he felt her grab the back of his shirt to stay close.

He wasn't sure if the ATF agents would follow them

out or not. He glanced back over his shoulder but didn't see them. Most likely they were discussing their next steps without him or Harper there to listen in.

Fine. He needed time to figure out his next steps too. Leading the way down the stairs to the first-floor landing, he moved slowly so that Harper could keep up. At the main door, he scanned the area before opening it.

He shielded her with his body as much as possible as they took the sidewalk down to Rhy's SUV. They were halfway there when he caught a hint of movement in his peripheral vision.

"Down!" He wrenched Harper down to the cold ground as the crack of gunfire echoed around them. He drew his weapon and returned fire, covering Harper as best as he could considering he had no idea how many bad guys were out there.

And where were the ATF agents?

"When I fire again, run for the SUV, understand?"

Harper's pale face gazed up at him.

When she nodded, he whispered, "Now!"

He fired at the corner of the apartment building, hoping to keep the shooter in place, seeking cover. Harper rose from her crouch and hurried toward the SUV. When she reached it, she opened the passenger door and crawled inside.

Banner and Perkins ran from the building. "Shooter on the northwest corner," he shouted.

The two agents split up, each heading in opposite directions with their weapons drawn. Steele ran for the car. He wanted to back them up, but his priority was to keep Harper safe. As he curled his body around hers, his gut twisted with agony.

Bringing her to the apartment had been a mistake.

CHAPTER NINE

She should be used to the sound of gunfire by now, but she wasn't. True to his word, Steele did his best to shield her with his body. But bullets could go through one person into the other, so she wasn't convinced they would get away from this unscathed. One of these times, a bullet would find its mark.

Why, Lord? Why did this keep happening?

She tried not to panic, to believe that God would keep her and her baby safe. Yet for some reason, praying didn't provide the comfort she desperately needed. After everything that had taken place in and outside her apartment, she felt certain she would either have her baby in prison or be killed.

And she didn't know which alternative scared her more.

"Get ready to climb into the SUV," Steele whispered in her ear.

She managed a nod. Her heart thundered so fast she worried about the impact on her baby. How much stress could one infant take?

"Now!"

Despite his warning, his command startled her. He moved back just enough for her to get upright. He yanked the car door open and stood behind her as she crawled inside.

"Stay down as much as possible."

"Okay." She had to duck sideways to get her head below the dashboard. This position wasn't comfortable either, but she didn't protest. Steele shut the door and exposed himself to danger by running around the front of the SUV and getting in behind the wheel.

Seconds later, he was pulling away from the curb, tires fishtailing on the icy road as they shot down the street.

"Brock, I need a clean vehicle ASAP," Steele said. "Gunfire broke out at Harper's apartment."

"Okay, where do you want to meet?"

"Neutral territory." He paused, then said, "How about Rosie's Diner?"

"Done. See you soon."

There was a long moment of silence as Steele continued driving. From the way she lurched from side to side, she could tell he was making several turns. The constant movement was making her ill.

"Can I sit up now?"

"Yes." His voice was still tight with concern. "Are you hurt?"

"I don't think so." Hard to tell since her body was tense with fear. She took several deep breaths before adding, "I'm fine. At least, physically."

He grimaced. "I understand. This hasn't been a very good morning."

"You think?" She couldn't hide her snide tone. "Those ATF agents believe I'm involved! And so do you."

"No, I don't." He cast her a quick look, before turning

his attention to the road. He was making so many turns she lost her sense of direction. "It's obvious to me the gun was planted in your dresser."

His words should have made her feel better. And maybe they did, at least a little. But in truth, Steele's believing in her didn't matter. He couldn't stop the ATF agents from arresting her.

She was no lawyer, but even she knew the feds trumped the state every time. She would be tried in a federal court in front of a federal judge.

And if convicted, sent to a federal penitentiary.

"Who knew I would be at the apartment?" The thought popped into her head. She turned to stare at Steele. "Just the four of us and Brock. Right?"

"Yeah, I see where you're going with this." His voice was subdued. "I had the same thought about the ATF agents setting you up. But if for some reason one of them wanted to set you up as being a willing participant in the gunrunning, instigating the shooting outside the building doesn't play into their hand. All that does is reinforce that Grotto's guys are trying to eliminate you as a threat."

"They could have hired someone." She couldn't get the image of Bryon Perkins's smug face out of her mind. "And eliminating me does play into their hands. The theory being that Grotto is snipping off loose ends."

"I don't know what to think," Steele admitted. "It seems unbelievable that Perkins or Banner is involved."

"Perkins thinks I'm responsible. It's not a stretch to think he's the one who set the trap."

"There's no proof he's involved," Steele said.

No proof she was either. Except for the gun that had been planted in her apartment. She turned away to look out her passenger window. The baby kicked, making her smile despite her grim situation.

Her baby was all that mattered. If he or she—she wished now she'd agreed to find out the baby's gender—survived this to live a long and happy life, then the pain and agony was well worth that outcome.

Even if that meant she wasn't around to share her baby's life.

A wave of sorrow hit hard, but she did her best to ignore it. Yes, she would suffer terribly if she couldn't be with her child. But she refused to be selfish.

From this point forward, she would remain focused on her baby's welfare. That would be all that mattered.

"Have you ever been to Rosie's Diner for breakfast or lunch?" Steele's question broke into her troubled thoughts.

"No." She didn't waste her money eating out. She planned her meals and brought a bag lunch to work each day.

"Rosie specializes in bakery."

She shrugged. "That's nice, but I'm not hungry."

"Harper, I'm on your side. I won't leave you until we get to the bottom of this."

Or until she was arrested, she thought but didn't say. "I know. I appreciate that."

Ten minutes later, Steele pulled into a small parking lot. The diner wasn't anything fancy, but based on the crowded lot, Rosie had a strong and loyal customer base.

"We may want to get lunch to go," Steele said as he shut down the engine.

"Whatever." She knew she sounded crabby and ungrateful. Because she was. Sitting there while Steve Banner and Bryon Perkins all but accused her of being a gunrunner or, worse, a murderer, had been unnerving.

"Wait for me." Steele pushed his driver's side door open.

She almost didn't but reminded herself that her baby's safety was important. When he came around to open the door for her, she turned and slid out.

"Harper, I'm sorry for what you've been through." His low voice made her long to rest against him. To be held in his arms.

"I know." She didn't try to smile. "Let's go inside."

He looked as if he wanted to say something more but simply nodded. He shut the car door, then walked with her inside. The scent of bacon mixed with cinnamon and nutmeg teased her senses. Despite her earlier comment about not being hungry, her stomach rumbled.

Steele stood there for a moment. A group of four people stood to leave one of the booths.

"Steele? Hey, how are you?" A blond-haired man grinned at them. "Take our booth. Rosie won't mind."

"Hi, Colin. I'm good, thanks. This is Harper Crane." Steele rested his hand on her back. "Harper, this is Colin Finnegan, his brother Aiden, his other brother Quinn, and Quinn's wife, Sami."

"Ah, nice to meet you." That was a lot of Finnegans. She hoped they didn't notice she was wearing Devon's maternity clothes.

"Nice to meet you too," Sami said with a warm smile.

"I hope you left some of Rosie's bakery for us," Steele teased. "I know Colin eats like a horse."

Colin laughed. "We all do, it's in our DNA. Nice to meet you, Harper. Steele, there might be one more cinnamon roll left for you, but I think you should do the gentlemanly thing and offer it to Harper."

"Stop teasing him." Quinn lightly punched Colin in the arm. "Everyone knows Rosie bakes all day long."

"Truth," Aiden agreed. "Enjoy your meal. We need to get going."

"Big plans?" Steele asked, edging past them toward the booth.

"They're helping us move into our new home." Aiden's brown eyes crinkled with a smile. "They lost a bet, so they get to be my muscle. Shelby and Eva are waiting for us in Oshkosh. Next weekend is our wedding. It's all going really fast, but we're thrilled."

"Sounds great. Try not to work too hard," Steele said.

"Yeah, yeah," Quinn groused. "Let's hit the road. The sooner we get this done, the better."

"Take care." The lighthearted teasing between the Finnegan siblings provided a sense of normalcy. As if she wasn't in danger from Grotto's gunmen. Then again, if she wasn't in danger, she never would have met Steele or any of the Finnegans.

She slid into the booth as a woman with red hair bustled toward them. "Ah, lass, let me clean the table first, won't ya?"

"Hey, Rosie," Steele greeted her.

"Why, if it isn't Steele Delaney! A fine Irish lad," Rosie added with a wink. "Are ya interested in my cinnamon rolls?"

"Yes, please." Steele grinned. "I knew Colin didn't eat them all."

Rosie let out a belly laugh as she cleaned the table, then hurried away. Harper leaned toward Steele. "Is she really from Ireland?"

"That's what she claims." He shrugged. "None of us

dare argue for fear she won't share her wonderful cooking with us."

Rosie returned with the biggest cinnamon rolls Harper had ever seen, along with two cups of coffee. "Oh, sorry, I only drink decaf," she protested.

"Aye, lass, I knew you were expecting. This is decaf, I promise." Rosie set the cup in front of her. "I'll be back to take the rest of your order."

"I can't eat all this," she protested.

"I'll eat what you don't," Steele said with a grin.

Five minutes later, Brock joined them. He dropped into the seat beside her and eyed her half-eaten cinnamon roll. "You finished with that?"

"Yes." She pushed the plate toward him.

"Fill me in," Brock said as he took a bite of the cinnamon roll.

Steele did so, not holding anything back. When he mentioned the SIG Sauer found in her underwear drawer, Brock scowled. "Obviously planted."

Considering Brock had been suspicious of her initially, his comment made her feel better. Not that it would matter in the long run. "What if Jake is the one setting me up?"

Both men stared at her. "You think so?" Steele asked.

She honestly didn't know what to think. "If not the ATF, then the only one who would hate me enough to do this is Jake."

"She has a point," Brock mused. "I hadn't considered that angle."

"Me either," Steele agreed. "But how is Jake pulling the strings to do all this?"

"Maybe he's lying about testifying against Grotto." Brock shrugged. "I don't know, but it's a possibility that should be easy to prove."

"How so?" Harper asked.

"He would have to have a hidden phone or some access to a computer to stay connected to Grotto, right?" Brock said.

"I was thinking it would be better if I spoke to Jake face-to-face," she said.

"No way," Steele said. "Not a chance."

She glanced at Brock who shook his head. "I'm not sure what good it would do." ·

"I'm the one being set up to take the fall." She couldn't hold back her anger. "I know Jake better than anyone else. If he's involved, I'll know."

"Not gonna happen," Steele repeated stubbornly.

She wanted to scream in frustration. "I need to use the restroom."

Brock slid out of the booth, giving her room. Tossing her napkin onto the table, she walked toward the restrooms, tempted to turn and head straight out the door.

And to keep walking until she'd left everything she'd ever known behind.

"SHE'S REALLY MAD," Brock said, resuming his seat.

"No kidding." Steele dragged his hands over his face. "There's no way we're going to set up a meeting between Harper and her ex-husband."

"Keep in mind, she is the one with the most to lose here." Brock finished her cinnamon roll, licking the icing off his fingers "She deserves some say in what happens next."

He didn't like it. Not one bit. But he understood her frustration. "What we need is a solid lead."

"The gun may give us something," Brock agreed.

"I need to call Rhy. Let him know the SUV has been compromised and about the new evidence against Harper."

"I'll return his SUV." Brock sighed, then said, "It's awfully convenient that the gun showed up at her place. Maybe we shouldn't trust the ATF guys."

That was his thought too. "I know they risked their lives at the warehouse shooting and, according to Flynn, saved his life. But if you could have seen how Perkins was gloating over the gun . . ." He didn't finish.

"Okay, then Harper has a point. If not the ATF guys, then Grotto could be orchestrating this with Feldman."

"Or maybe Grotto is doing this on his own," Steele mused. "Maybe he thinks Feldman was arrested because Harper found something incriminating?"

"That's possible." Brock glanced toward the restrooms. "If she doesn't come back soon, you need to check on her."

Steele slouched back in the booth. "You really think her meeting with Feldman is a good idea?"

"I didn't at first, but now? Maybe." When Steele scowled, Brock quickly added, "Feldman is in custody. He can't hurt her."

He wasn't convinced that was true. Feldman had hurt her, physically and emotionally. The last thing he wanted was for her to be hurt all over again.

As if the recent events surrounding the planted gun and the shooting weren't bad enough, she wanted to face the lion in his den.

He abruptly stood, then paused when he saw Harper returning to the table. Her eyes looked slightly puffy, as if she'd been crying. He wanted to ask if she was okay, but that seemed silly.

She wasn't okay. Would not be okay until they'd found and arrested Grotto and whoever he was working with.

"I'm sorry," he murmured, placing a hand on her arm. "I'll see what Rhy thinks about you speaking with your ex. It's not my call, the ATF has to agree too. Your ex is currently in their custody."

She grimaced. "I hadn't thought of that. But thanks, Steele. I appreciate you asking Rhy."

He longed to pull her close, but Rosie chose that moment to return to their table. She brought another large cinnamon roll for Brock.

"Will ya be having breakfast then too?" Rosie asked.

"Not for us, Rosie." Steele drew Harper into the seat beside him. "Brock can stay and eat if he's hungry."

"Of course, I'm hungry," Brock shot back. "But where are you going?"

"Back to the hotel." He didn't have to say the exact location, Brock knew they'd been staying at the City Central Hotel. He glanced at Harper. "Did you want to order lunch to go?"

"Sure, I guess." She didn't sound enthusiastic. He knew the point of the ATF needing to agree to her meeting with Feldman had squashed her hopes of making progress.

When Rosie returned, he and Harper ordered lunch to go, while Brock ordered the lumberjack's breakfast.

Less than an hour later, he and Harper were heading outside to the SUV Brock had rented for them. Brock had agreed to cover the bill at Rosie's too, and Steele was getting a little worried about how much money they were going through in their quest to keep Harper and her baby safe.

Not that he minded spending it on her, but Brock and Rhy and the others shouldn't have to foot the bill.

"You believe the City Central Hotel is safe?" Harper asked as he left the jam-packed parking lot.

"Yes. There are only two people who know we're

staying there, Brock and Rhy." He was glad he hadn't given the location to the ATF agents. "We can trust them both."

"Okay." She smoothed her hands over her stomach as he took a winding route back to the hotel. "It would be nice to feel safe again."

Words no pregnant woman should have to say, he thought grimly. Losing his sister and Monique had been difficult, but he would feel just as awful if something terrible happened to Harper and her baby. He decided to call Rhy once they were back at the hotel. Better than having the conversation through the SUV's wireless connection.

As before, he parked way in the back corner of the parking lot, near the side entrance. Carrying their to-go bags, he led her inside. Harper still had the small backpack, too, having hung onto it during the shooting.

Once he'd tucked their meals inside the small fridge, he held out his hand for the backpack. "Do you mind if I just make sure there isn't a tracking device?"

She handed it over. "I guess privacy doesn't matter anymore."

He felt bad going through her personal things. There was no device hidden inside, so he handed it back. "Sorry about that. It's just better to be safe than sorry."

She turned away. "I'm going to take a shower."

He let her go, understanding she needed time alone. No matter how many times he'd tried to reassure her that he believed in her innocence, there was no denying the shock he'd felt upon seeing that gun. And the photograph of her and Dillweed.

Dropping onto the sofa, he called Rhy. "I'm sorry to say your SUV was burned."

"You mean by fire?" Rhy asked in shock.

"No, sorry. I meant I used it to go to Harper's apartment, and gunfire rang out. I left it with Brock, he'll return it when he's done stuffing his face."

"Oh, that's fine." Rhy sounded relieved. "But why would you go to Harper's apartment?"

He filled his boss in on the recent events. When he came to the part where the ATF found a SIG Sauer in her underwear drawer, Rhy snorted.

"You've got to be kidding me," Rhy said in disgust.

It was heartening to know the members of the tactical team believed in Harper too. It wasn't just him being blind because he cared about her. "Yeah, that's what I said."

"We have proof that her apartment was breached to place a tracking device in her shoe and car. No reason they couldn't plant a gun too."

"Yeah, I pointed that out, too. But, Rhy, her shoes, purse, and coat were left behind in the American Lodge. Technically, all you have is my word that I saw it."

"No, we have the device," Rhy assured him. "The crime scene techs have it at the lab. They found one in her purse too. Looks like the coat was clean."

That was a relief. "Good. That should help."

"What's the end game?" Rhy asked. "I mean, they should either frame her or kill her. Doing both makes no sense. First there's an attempted kidnapping, then several shooting incidents, then planting evidence. There's no logical pattern."

"I know, the shotgun approach is bugging me too." He told Rhy about Harper's request to meet with her ex-husband face-to-face.

His boss whistled. "Not sure the ATF will go along with that."

"I know, but what do you think?" If Steele were honest,

he'd admit he didn't trust his instincts when it came to Harper.

"I think she's right in saying she knows him better than we do. It can't hurt."

"Okay, thanks." Steele would go along with the plan since the ATF had to approve the meeting anyway.

"Do you need more cash?" Rhy asked. "Or any other kind of support?"

"I'm good. But if you hear anything, please keep me in the loop. I'm concerned the ATF will freeze me out now that they've found the gun."

"I will. But I'm sure they're smart enough to realize that Harper is being framed," Rhy assured him.

Banner? Yes. Perkins? Not so much. "Take care, Rhy." He disconnected from the call.

He stood and paced, listening at Harper's bedroom door for a moment, before moving on. He hated to admit that the investigation was at a standstill. Unless something popped with the evidence they'd collected so far, there wasn't anything more he could do.

Except arrange the meeting between Harper and Feldman.

He didn't want to do it. He paced again, trying to come up with another plan.

When his phone rang, he grimaced when he recognized Banner's number. Glancing at Harper's bedroom door, he was glad it was still closed. He quickly touched the talk button. "What's up?"

"Where are you?" Banner asked.

"Safe. What's going on? Did you find the shooter?"

"No, but we have techs reviewing street camera video," Banner said. "We also put a rush on the ballistics testing of the SIG found in the apartment."

His gut clenched. "Any prints on the weapon?"

There was a slight hesitation. "No prints, seems as if the gun was wiped clean. But the tech just informed me the gun is a match for the slug found embedded in Ellis Starkey's body. It's the murder weapon."

The news was a sucker punch to the gut. He sank onto the sofa. "That's interesting. I'm convinced Grotto placed it there."

There was a long pause from Banner. "Look, Delaney, I know how you feel. But we can't ignore the evidence."

"You mean the planted evidence." He couldn't hold back the anger. "Come on, Banner, think about it. If Harper had used the weapon to kill Starkey and wiped her prints off, why would she keep it in her apartment? Why not toss it in Lake Michigan?"

Hearing a gasp, he turned to see Harper standing in the doorway, her hand over her mouth. He winced, realizing he'd been practically shouting at Banner.

"I know, it's definitely suspicious," Banner agreed. "I just thought you should know. We'd like to formally ask Harper not to leave the area."

His gut clenched again. That almost sounded like they were planning to arrest her. "Fine. Anything else?"

"No. Just keep in touch, okay?" With that, Banner disconnected from the call.

"When are they coming to get me?" Harper asked.

"They're not." He tossed his phone aside and rose to his feet. He crossed over to take her hands in his. "It's clearly a setup. Banner and Perkins don't know where we are, and I plan to keep it that way."

She nodded, her gaze downcast. The way she accepted her imminent arrest broke his heart. He pulled her into his arms, wishing he could put her on a plane and fly to a remote island in the middle of the ocean. Anything to keep her safe.

To his surprise, she wrapped her arms around his waist and held on tight. He gathered her closer still, desperate to reassure her that she was safe with him.

"Thanks for believing in me." Her voice was muffled against his shirt.

"Always." He meant it, even though as a cop he shouldn't. Logically, anything was possible.

When Harper lifted her head, her eyes were bright with tears. He held her gaze, then lowered his head to capture her lush mouth with his.

Kissing her the way he'd only dreamed about.

CHAPTER TEN

Harper lost herself in the wonder of Steele's kiss. It seemed like so long since she'd felt cherished. And his kiss was better than anything she'd experienced in her life. But when her baby kicked him in the stomach, he broke off their embrace, glancing down at her belly as if embarrassed.

"I—uh," he faltered, raked his hand through his hair, then said, "I hope I didn't make you feel uncomfortable."

"No, you didn't." She'd moved beyond what Jake had done. Focusing instead on the baby she loved more than anything.

Watching Steele flounder almost made her smile. She wondered what he would do if she kissed him again. Then the reality of her situation crashed over her. What was she thinking kissing Steele? Any minute now, the ATF agents would issue a warrant for her arrest.

This—was nothing more than a brief interlude. A very nice, wonderful interlude.

But temporary just the same.

"Come sit down." He took a step backward, seeming to

look everywhere but at her. "How are your feet holding up?"

"Fine." Her blistered feet were the least of her worries. She reminded herself that Steele could have any woman he wanted. He was tall, dark, and handsome. There was no reason to believe he'd be interested in a pregnant woman like her or a ready-made family.

"Let me know when you'd like to eat lunch," he said.

"Food can wait. What did Banner say?" She'd only heard Steele's side of the conversation. The way he'd vehemently supported her had been sweet. Maybe she'd been too hard on him during the apartment search. He had obviously been as surprised by their finding the gun as she was.

"I think you heard most of it." He dropped into the chair adjacent to the sofa. "The SIG was used to kill Ellis Starkey. But there were no fingerprints on the gun, indicating the shooter wiped it clean or used gloves."

"There is no reason for me to kill Ellis." She found it hard to believe she was even saying it. "I told you he was nice to me." She remembered what he'd said about how any normal shooter would toss the gun into Lake Michigan. "The only reason the gun was found in my apartment was because someone put it there."

"I agree." He smiled. "Try not to worry about it."

Impossible, but she nodded. She'd hoped her shower would make her feel better, but it was Steele's kiss that had brought a hint of peace. "You know, I still think it's odd that the gun was in my dresser drawer."

"Because that's not where you would have hidden it?" Steele asked.

"No, but since the goal was to frame me, why not put it in the blue vase?"

Steele frowned. "They looked inside the blue vase. There was nothing but the plastic flowers."

"I know that, but it's the vase Ellis gave me." She sighed. "The one he claimed was from the warehouse. It has a small chip, so he said they couldn't sell it. I just set it near the wall, where the chip wasn't visible."

"Wait a minute, Starkey gave you a vase?" Steele looked surprised.

"It wasn't some big romantic gesture or anything," she quickly explained. "Ellis wasn't a flirt. I truly believe he thought I'd like to have it."

"Was this after you moved into the apartment?" Steele frowned. "I thought you hadn't seen him for a few weeks before you left Feldman."

"No, I took the vase with me when I moved." She remembered feeling a little foolish for bringing it along. "I didn't want anything Jake gave me, but the vase added a little color to the place." Really, it was the flowers that she'd enjoyed the most.

"You're sure Starkey was never in your apartment?" He pressed. "Maybe you mixed up your dates."

She clenched her jaw. "I'm sure. I have never lied to you, Steele. Not once. Just because Ellis was nice to me didn't make him my close confidant. Just the opposite. I figured anything I told him would end up going straight to Jake. Ellis was loyal to him. Why? I have no idea."

"Okay, okay." He held up his hand. "It's just that you never mentioned the blue vase before."

Hadn't she? Maybe not. "I was only saying that if Jake was behind this, he probably would have mentioned the vase as a good hiding spot."

"Yeah, maybe." He appeared lost in thought as if trying to envision the vase.

"Perkins searched it, remember? It was empty." She wished she hadn't brought up how Ellis had brought it home for her. At the time, she'd been grateful for the little bit of compassion. A gift with no strings attached.

And wasn't that pathetic? She'd made a mess of her life, that was for sure. Mistakes that were coming back to haunt her in a big way.

All the reason not to let her feelings for Steele cloud her judgment. Steele seemed nice and caring, but he could have a dark side. Or some other terrible habit that she wasn't aware of yet.

No one was perfect.

"Yeah, okay. I just wish I could look at the vase again," he murmured. "If not for the shooting incident, I'd go back and grab it."

She stifled a sigh. "It's just a vase. Trust me, there's nothing special about it. During the summer months, I fill it with water for the wildflowers I pick on my early morning walks at Greenland Park before work. I can't afford to buy flowers in the winter, so I use the plastic ones instead. Besides, if there was anything inside, the ATF guys would have found it."

That finally seemed to convince him to let it go. "Okay, that makes sense."

"We should probably eat." She wasn't hungry, but it was something to do. Anything to avoid thinking about that kiss.

"Count me in." He rose to his feet and crossed the room. He unpacked the large to-go bag, frowning a bit. "You only ordered a salad."

"That's all I wanted." She was gaining more than enough weight, at least according to her last doctor's appointment. She joined him at the table. "Hey, we didn't order another cinnamon roll."

"Looks like Rosie packed extra." He smiled. "She's pretty awesome."

"Yes, the menu was larger than I expected." Her experience with restaurants was limited. Her parents never had much money, so they rarely went out. And living with Jake hadn't exactly been a step up. "Sounds like the Finnegans are big fans too."

"They are," Steele agreed. "That's how I learned about the place. Apparently, Colin is some sort of frustrated chef."

"Funny," she said with a smile.

He turned to look at her, and it took a moment for her to realize he was waiting for her to say grace.

She bowed her head, searching for God's presence. Despite the hardships she faced, and the possible arrest looming on the horizon, she knew He was still watching out for her. "Lord Jesus, we are thankful for this food we are about to eat. Bless Rosie's business, and please continue to keep all police officers safe in Your care. Amen."

"Amen," Steele said. "And, Lord, please keep Harper and her precious baby safe in Your care too. Amen."

For a moment, she couldn't speak. Tears that had nothing to do with hormones pricked her eyes. "Thank you, Steele."

"I'm here for you," he repeated.

She nodded and picked up her plastic fork. The Cobb salad was chock-full of protein, so she forced herself to eat. For the sake of her baby.

"Do you know if you're having a boy or a girl?" Steele asked.

She shook her head. "No. I wanted it to be a surprise." She toyed with the grilled chicken in her salad. "With everything going on, I wish I did know one way or the other."

"Have you picked out names?"

She had toyed with a few but hadn't settled on anything. "Not yet." She glanced at him. "I know that must sound like I'm not excited about this pregnancy, but I am." She flushed, and added, "I keep thinking that the perfect name will come to me once he or she is born."

"I understand."

She speared a cherry tomato. "You've never married? Had kids?" A little late to be asking after that sizzling kiss.

"Nope." He shrugged. "Two years ago, my girlfriend Monique was killed by a drunk driver. I also lost my older sister when I was in high school. She was killed by her boyfriend."

Her eyes widened in horror. "That's terrible. I'm so sorry for your losses."

"Yeah. I was single-minded in becoming a cop, taking bad guys off the street."

"I can understand that," she said. "I'm sorry about your sister. And your girlfriend."

"Thanks. It was a long time ago, and the good news is that Amelia's boyfriend was arrested and thrown in jail. The drunk driver was arrested too. Knowing that justice was done in both cases helps a little."

"And I'm sure both your sister and your girlfriend are in heaven now."

He nodded slowly. "I hadn't considered that, but yeah. I'd like to think so."

She wanted to press on the issue of his faith but let it go. They ate in silence for a while. The rest of the day loomed ahead of them. Considering she was on borrowed time, about to be arrested at any moment, her thoughts turned back to her ex.

"I really need to talk to Jake."

He winced and shook his head. "I don't see how anything good could come out of that."

"What else am I supposed to do? Sit here and wait for the ATF to slap cuffs around my wrists?" She bit back her impatience. "Do you have a better idea?"

He finished his wrap, then balled up the garbage, shooting it like a basketball into the container in the corner. "Not really. And you're not going to be arrested, Harper. Banner is leaning toward this being a setup."

Banner, but not Perkins. "It doesn't matter. They're going to want to tie this case up sooner than later."

"I ran the idea past Rhy," he admitted. "He'll discuss it with ATF agents. Your ex-husband is in their custody, so the final decision is out of my hands."

He'd spoken to Rhy? That surprised her, but she was glad he'd taken her request seriously. She pushed her half-eaten salad away. Despite the meeting being her idea, her stomach churned at the thought of coming face-to-face with Jake.

Yet she would do that and more if it meant keeping her unborn child safe.

STEELE MOVED AWAY from the kitchenette, shoving his hands into his pockets to keep from reaching for Harper. The way she kept referring to her imminent arrest bothered him.

Deep down, he knew she was mentally preparing herself for the worst. And he even understood it to some extent. Being there when the ATF uncovered the gun in her apartment had been horrible for her. She didn't want to find herself in that situation again.

He didn't either. But that didn't mean he was on board with Harper facing off with Feldman.

The need to do something constructive sent him pacing again. This sitting around, breathing in Harper's sweet scent, was killing him. He'd rather face another warehouse shooting than sit here pretending he didn't want to kiss her again.

The shooting at her apartment bugged him. She was wearing borrowed clothes, new shoes, and didn't have a purse or a phone. There's no way they were tailed there in Rhy's SUV either.

Had the ATF agents set them up? No, the more likely scenario was that Grotto had someone watching the place. That person had seen them go inside and had set up an ambush, waiting for them to come out.

"What are you thinking?" Harper asked.

"The incident outside your apartment." He paused midstride, turning to look at her. "Did you see the shooter?"

"No. I heard the gunshot but didn't see anyone."

That made sense as he'd thought the gunman was standing on his side of the building. "I'm a little shocked they missed."

Her eyes widened. "That's a good thing."

"Yeah, but the shooter was close enough that he could have easily killed me." A thug reluctant to shoot him? Not likely. Going back over the incident in his mind, he realized he'd been standing in front of Harper. Maybe the goal had been to get him to move, opening her up for a shot.

Why? That was the sticking point. Harper seemed to think both Feldman and Grotto might have come after her to seek revenge. That was certainly the motive behind his sister's murder. Her ex-boyfriend couldn't stand the idea of being replaced.

But these attacks weren't up close and personal. Except maybe for the first one, the attempted abduction. In his experience as a cop, personal attacks were not carried out from afar.

They'd thoroughly questioned her, and she claimed she didn't know anything.

But what if there was something that she knew but didn't understand the significance behind it? The image of her talking to Dillweed outside her church flashed in his mind.

He spun on his heel. "Harper, I need you to look at more pictures." Crossing the room, he returned to the small table.

She'd cleared the rest of their garbage away, so he drew the computer over and booted it up.

"What kind of pictures?" She hovered near his right shoulder.

Close enough to kiss.

Enough. Stay focused! He kept his gaze locked on the computer screen, but the rest of his senses were in tune with her. He should feel guilty for being attracted to her, like he was being untrue to Monique's memory, but he didn't.

He cleared his throat. "You met and spoke to a man from your church who introduced himself as Glenn Vice. Only he was really a known gunrunner, Kenny Dillon, a.k.a. Dillweed."

"Yes, that's true." She dropped into a chair. "You mentioned Kenny was one of the three men killed at the warehouse shooting."

"Exactly. I asked you about their names to see if they sounded familiar. But now I need you to look at their faces." His fingers flew across the keyboard, queuing up a search of the other two perps, Arlo Carbine and Perro Segura, also known as Carbo and Parrott.

It took a minute for him to bring them up on the screen. He positioned the two mug shots side by side, then turned the computer toward her. "Either of these guys look familiar?"

She studied the screen for several minutes.

With a heavy sigh, she shook her head. "I don't recognize either of them." She paused, then tapped Parrott's picture. "He might be vaguely familiar. Like maybe I saw him a long time ago. But I can't pinpoint when or where. Possibly with Jake?"

"At your place? Or somewhere else?"

"I don't know." She frowned. "Honestly, the more I look at him, the less confident I am that I saw him before. I wouldn't be able to swear to it in court or anything."

He hid his disappointment. "Any chance one of them was hanging around Kenny in church?"

She continued looking at the mug shots. "If he was, I didn't notice. I remember Glenn—er, Kenny being alone. Like I was." Her cheeks went pink. "I know that sounds pathetic, but I had thought maybe he could be a friend."

"It's not pathetic to want friends." Steele didn't know what he'd do without his fellow teammates and the rest of the Finnegans. They were more than just friends to him; they were his extended family. The only family he had in the world. "It's natural. Humans are social by nature."

She turned to look at him. "Thanks for saying that. I still feel foolish for believing he was interested." She shook her head. "I wish I could be more help."

"You're doing fine." He turned the computer back. "I'll keep poking around a bit. Maybe I'll find something."

"Okay." She sat for a moment, then rose and moved

away. He continued searching social media sites but didn't find anything interesting.

On a whim, he typed in the name Glenn Vice. To his surprise, there were several of them on social media. He scanned the list until he saw a picture that looked an awful lot like Kenny Dillon.

Clicking on the image, he was stunned to see that there was an entire fake profile that had been created for Glenn Vice. Supposedly, the guy was a Christian, attended church, and worked as an accountant at Peterson and Kline.

"Harper?" He waved for her to come back to the table. "Did you search on Vice at all? Did you find this profile?"

"No, that didn't occur to me." She sucked in a harsh breath. "All of that is fake? Right down to his job as an accountant?"

"Yes." He wondered if Dillweed had given up after that first meeting or if he'd simply lost interest in the plan of courting her long enough to draw her into a trap. Personally, he thought that would have worked far better than the amateur attempt to snatch her off the sidewalk outside the law offices.

He mentally reviewed the timing. When exactly had Feldman gotten beat up? Two months ago?

About the same time as Dillweed gave up pretending to be Glenn Vice? Is that when the plan had changed? The shoot-out at the warehouse had taken place two weeks ago. Two weeks in which they'd tried to find Tommy Grotto and Waylon Brooks.

And following Harper in case one of them reached out to her. Which they had, just not in the way they'd anticipated.

The Glenn Vice plan to set up Harper had certainly

died with Kenny Dillon's death. That was likely the reason they'd resorted to a stop-and-grab attempt.

There were so many missing pieces in this puzzle it wasn't funny. Kenny Dillon had pretended to attend church, striking up a friendly conversation with Harper for a reason.

He reached for his phone to call Banner, then stopped himself before making the call. No reason to bring the ATF agents along with every step he made. In fact, all he had was supposition and theory.

This entire case was supposition and theory. If not for the fifty guns found inside the warehouse, he'd think they were chasing smoke signals.

He spent another fifteen minutes pouring through Glenn Vice's social media account. The guy had been careful, he'd give him that much. All the people he'd friended appeared to attend the same church as Harper.

Obviously, there were no links to Grotto or Brooks. Or Feldman.

When his phone rang, he froze when he saw Banner's number. He ignored the call before he could talk himself out of it.

As if not talking to the ATF would prevent them from continuing to work the case.

He quickly picked up the phone and called Raelyn. "Hey, do you have an update?"

"You mean on the Starkey murder?" Rae asked.

"Yes. I'm sure you heard the weapon was found."

"I did." She hesitated, then said, "I don't believe Harper Crane killed Starkey. And I think the ME agrees with us."

He liked the sound of that, even if it was almost too good to be true. "Care to explain?"

"I spent a fair amount of time with the ME during the

autopsy." Attending autopsies was never fun, but to her credit, Rae didn't shy away from the gruesome job. Neither did Jina nor Cassidy, the other female officers on the team. "He thinks the killer was a tall male based on the trajectory of the bullet. There was no evidence Starkey was kneeling, so he was standing upright, his chin planted firmly against his chest as the shot was fired. That means the shooter was taller than Harper."

"Okay, go on." He was encouraged by the news.

"There's also the fact that the murder took place somewhere else. Starkey was literally tossed into the dumpster like garbage."

His heart sank. "Even one strong guy couldn't do that. It would take two people to get him up and inside. That doesn't exonerate Harper. Not if she had help."

"Depends on the killer," Rae admitted. "But with Harper being short and pregnant, she'd be little to no help in dumping the body."

Maybe. He tried to take comfort in the ME's opinion. "That sounds good, Rae. Thanks for the information."

"How is she?" Rae asked.

He glanced at Harper, who was sitting with her eyes closed making circles on her pregnant belly. "Hanging in there."

"Keep her safe, Steele. I have a bad feeling about this case."

"You and me both." His phone rang again. A glance at the screen indicated the call was from Steve Banner. He sighed. "This is the ATF. I have to go."

"Later." Rae ended the call.

He pressed the button to answer the call. "Hey, Steve. I was on the other line with Raelyn. What's going on?"

"I just heard from Finnegan." Banner didn't beat

around the bush. "Sounds like Ms. Crane is interested in a face-to-face meeting with her ex-husband."

He really, really wished he hadn't mentioned it to Rhy. "She is, yes." He could feel Harper's gaze on him, her previous Zen mode having vanished.

"Why?"

It was a good question. He considered the best way to respond. "She thinks her ex-husband is framing her for the murder of Ellis Starkey out of a deep-seated revenge."

"Impossible," Banner shot back. "He's had no contact with anyone outside of the safe house."

"And you know that for sure?"

"Yes, there are two ATF agents sitting on him in Chicago," Banner said. "I'm telling you, he's not responsible."

He almost hoped Banner would deny the request. "Look, I'm just telling you what she's thinking. She pointed out that she knows her ex-husband better than anyone else. If you're not on board with the plan, that's fine. I'll let her know."

"I didn't say that," Banner protested. "I'm just trying to understand what's going on."

"Join the club, we'd like to know that too." He wasn't about to give away the ME's theory of how Starkey had been killed. For one thing, there were always expert opinions that would try to sway a jury one way or the other.

But more importantly, Banner and Perkins should do their own legwork.

"Okay, we'll arrange a meeting." Banner's concession caught him off guard.

"When?" He glanced at his watch. Getting to Chicago or bringing Feldman here would take at least two hours if not more.

"Tomorrow late morning. I'll let you know the details later."

"Fine." He ended the call.

"He agreed?" Harper sounded surprised.

"Yeah." The barbecued chicken swirled in his gut. He didn't like it. And he found himself hoping and praying something would happen between now and the morning to prevent this meeting from taking place.

CHAPTER ELEVEN

Even though it had been her idea to meet with Jake, a shiver of apprehension slid down her spine. Harper told herself to get over it. She would face her ex multiple times if that would help them figure out who was trying to frame her.

"There's still time for you to change your mind," Steele said.

She managed a smile. "I won't. Thanks for arranging it."

"Yeah, against my better judgment," he muttered.

Maybe so, but it was a step forward. It seemed like all they were doing was running from one crisis to the next. Now that this meeting was set up, though, the rest of the day loomed before them.

She needed to do something. To stay busy. Anything to keep from ruminating over the upcoming meeting with her ex-husband.

An idea struck, so she pulled out her disposable phone.

"What are you doing?" Steele asked.

"Calling my boss." Without giving him time to protest, she quickly punched in the numbers and waited for someone to answer. Normally, that would be her job. But in her absence, the lawyers and paralegals would take turns.

"Gibson and Roberts," a deep male voice answered. She was a little surprised to recognize Trent's voice on the other end of the line.

"Trent, it's Harper."

"I tried to call on you the other day, but your voice mail box was full." He almost sounded suspicious.

"Oh, yes, well, I lost my phone, remember? I gave you this number." She didn't like lying, but it was easier than explaining about the constant gunfire and tracking devices. Oh, and let's not forget being framed for murder. If anyone had told her this would happen, she'd have laughed like crazy. Only she wasn't laughing now. "Do you want to make a note of it again?"

"Yeah, yeah. I do remember now." Trent was silent for a moment as he recorded the phone number, then asked, "How are you doing? Everything okay?"

"Sure. Listen, I'm sitting around with nothing to do. What do you think about letting me work from home for a day or two?" She saw Steele frown but ignored him, holding her breath and waiting for her boss to respond.

"Yeah, I guess we could do that," he finally agreed. "But just for a day or two, Harper. I could use your help here in the office more so than working remotely."

"I know, and I'm really sorry for the inconvenience." It wasn't her fault someone tried to kidnap her, but then again, it wasn't Trent's fault either. "I'll use this time to get caught up on billing and other routine tasks. And if you need something specific, all you need to do is call. I'll help out any way I can."

"That would be great." There was another pause, then Trent spoke again to someone in the background. "Yes, I'll be right there. Have a seat." Then he said to Harper, "I have to go. Doing more trial prep today."

"That's fine. Thanks, Trent." She disconnected from the call.

"You should have talked to me about this plan of yours," Steele said.

"Why? There's nothing going on this afternoon, is there?" She crossed over to the table. "I'll need to use the computer for a while."

"Yeah, that's what I mean." His tone came across as disgruntled. "I can't use it if you're working remotely."

"You said yourself that you weren't finding anything." She wasn't going to apologize for wanting to keep her job and to stay busy. "I can't keep burning vacation time, Steele. I'll need every day possible for time off after I deliver my baby."

He sighed and nodded. "Okay, fine. I have my phone. Go ahead and do your thing."

She quickly logged on to the computer. At first, she was worried the hotel internet wouldn't work, but the connection went through. Within minutes, she was in her email.

There were dozens of unread messages, as always. Many were just informational, but she quickly went through them, weeding through those that could be dealt with later and answering any that were urgent.

It felt good to be useful, to do something constructive. She should have thought of this earlier. Yet even as that idea flitted through her mind, she realized that up until the past twenty-four hours, she hadn't been safe in one place long enough to do anything. Much less work.

When she'd finished her emails, she pulled up the billable hours spreadsheet that the lawyers kept updated for her. She began collating the data, not surprised to note Neil

Otterson had the most billable hours for the past two weeks.

As they were prepping for his upcoming trial, she knew that number was likely to grow exponentially. One thing Trent Gibson never skimped on was trial prep with witnesses. Especially if there was a possibility of Neil himself testifying in his own defense.

Normally, that was only done as a last resort. Yet Trent always wanted his clients to be prepared in case they had to switch up their trial strategy.

Steele crossed behind her to get more coffee, then paused to glance over her shoulder. She instinctively minimized the screen.

"Wow, you're quite the spreadsheet guru," he said with admiration. "I can barely manage reports in Word."

"Only because I taught myself, practicing during the evening hours," she admitted. "I knew it was a requirement for this job."

"What are you working on?"

"Ah, billing stuff." She twisted in her seat to glance up at him. "I'm sorry, Steele, but this is confidential. You know, attorney-client privilege."

"I didn't think billable hours counted in attorney-client privilege," Steele replied.

"It's still confidential." Maybe it did, and maybe it didn't. Either way, she didn't feel right letting him see. "Please, Steele."

"Of course." He moved on, returning to the living room sofa. "Let me know when you're ready for dinner."

As she worked, she frowned when she saw what appeared to be duplicate billing hours for Neil Otterson. A mistake? Most likely. Especially since she'd been gone for a few days.

She straightened out the data and then created an invoice. Once that was ready, she sent it to Trent for approval. The dollar amount was huge, but she was used to seeing the outrageous prices the attorneys charged for their services. Again, she considered herself fortunate to work for a successful attorney that could afford to pay her a decent salary.

After a moment's hesitation, she went back to the prior month's billing. That amount seemed higher too. She sat back in her seat, wondering if the double billing was done on purpose. Sometimes, if both Trent Gibson and his partner Earl Roberts worked together on a case, they did bill for both attorneys' services. But usually there was a note indicating that. There wasn't any note in the current spreadsheet.

She decided to leave the current invoice she sent to Trent alone. If it was wrong, he'd tell her. Trent was good about double-checking things. Especially when it came to the firm's bottom line.

"Harper?" Steele clicked on a light, making her blink. She was so engrossed in her work she hadn't realized how many hours had passed. Darkness had fallen outside. "You really need to eat. You barely ate half your salad at lunch."

"Okay." She couldn't deny feeling hungry. "Place our order while I finish this up, will you?"

He pushed the menu toward her. As if she didn't have it memorized already. The options were limited.

"I'll have the grilled chicken sandwich, thanks." She listened to Steele place the order as she finished updating the file she was working on. As she logged off, she felt a sense of accomplishment. Not only had she saved herself four hours of vacation time, she'd gotten caught up on her emails.

"You were pretty intense," Steele said with a wry smile. "You like all that legal stuff, huh?"

"It's interesting." She flushed at the idea of him watching her. She closed the computer and pushed it out of the way. "I like to keep busy."

"Me too." He sighed. "It goes against the grain to sit here doing nothing while the rest of the team is working the case."

"I can imagine." Obviously, Steele was a man of action. Not prone to sitting around all day like she was. "Maybe meeting with Jake will shake something loose."

"I doubt it." He frowned, and just like that, the camaraderie between them fizzled out. "I still think it's a bad idea."

He could think what he wanted. She wasn't going to change her mind.

A knock at their door had her jumping in her seat. Okay, she wasn't going to change her mind, but that didn't mean she wasn't on edge. Steele crossed over to check through the peephole before opening the door to take the tray.

The scent of french fries made her mouth water. They weren't healthy, but she didn't care. Returning to some level of normalcy even for a few hours had brought her appetite back.

Steele uncovered their plates, then sat beside her. She was about to say grace, but Steele surprised her by taking her hand.

"Dear Lord, thank You for this food we're about to eat. We ask that You continue to keep us all safe in Your care, the entire tactical team but especially Harper and her unborn child. Amen."

"Amen." Her voice was husky with emotion. She

glanced at their joined hands, then up at Steele. "That was nice."

"We need God's protection now more than ever." He gently squeezed her hand, then released her to cut his chicken sandwich in half.

He was right, but the fact that he'd even bothered to pray for her was humbling. She almost wished she'd met Steele before she'd married Jake. But no, she'd been blessed with this baby. She wouldn't regret that.

But this time with Steele only reinforced the truth. That a husband and more children was something she'd never have.

STEELE FORCED HIMSELF TO EAT. His nerves were stretched to the breaking point. Not because of the danger, they were safe here. But this togetherness with Harper was wearing on him.

He hadn't truly appreciated what Joe had gone through last month while protecting Elly. It had been obvious that Joe was falling for Rhy's younger sister, talk about playing with fire. He'd warned Joe from getting too involved, yet here he was doing the exact same thing. The only difference was that Joe and Elly were engaged to be married. The entire team had been invited to their wedding next month. The Finnegans didn't wait around, they jumped right into marriage without hesitation.

Watching Harper work today should have been boring, like watching paint dry.

But it wasn't.

He'd spent some time following up with Rae and Brock about the evidence they'd found in the brown SUV and the various shooting scenes. Unfortunately, the crime scene techs hadn't uncovered anything new.

The planted murder weapon had nagged at him all afternoon. He went back and forth between suspecting the ATF agents of planting it to Tommy Grotto doing the deed himself. He always came back to the idea that the ATF agents wouldn't be so stupid as to put the gun there, then set themselves up as the cops who found it.

Which left Tommy Grotto or his buddy Waylon Brooks. He'd also wondered why the information Harper's ex-husband had given the ATF agents hadn't yielded any fruit. In his opinion, if Feldman was being straight with them, they'd have one or the other in custody by now.

Preferably both.

Something to discuss tomorrow during the meeting. He'd already asked Brock to ride along with them to the precinct. He knew the meeting wouldn't take place until late morning, as the ATF agents would need to transport Feldman here from Chicago, but he planned to get Harper there early. If nothing else, he wanted some time to talk to Rhy and Joe about their next steps.

"That was good, Steele. Thanks." Harper stacked her dishes, then yawned. "I'm sorry, but I need to get some sleep."

"That's fine." He took the tray from her fingers. "I'll deal with this. Go relax, Harper. It's been a long day."

"No kidding," she murmured. She flashed a brief smile, then walked toward her bedroom.

He finished eating, then set the tray outside their door. The hotel was quiet, which was probably a good thing. He felt too restless to sleep, so he went back to pacing the room.

It was nice to have a safe place for Harper, but the inactivity was driving him nuts. They couldn't just hang out in hotel rooms forever. They needed a plan to draw the shooter out into the open. Not that he intended to use Harper as bait, but maybe a female officer could be used as her double? The more he'd thought about it, the more he'd warmed to the idea.

Jina had long blond hair too. Her features were more angular than Harper's, but if she wore her hair down and had a pillow tucked under her clothes to fake a pregnancy, anyone watching her from a distance might believe she's Harper.

It could work. Especially if there was only a small handful of people who knew about the trap. Specifically, the members of the tactical team and no one else.

Not even the ATF agents.

He'd decided not to mention the idea to Harper until he had buy-in from the upper brass. He doubted Harper would like it, even if it meant getting their hands on the shooter. But he wasn't sure that Rhy would go along with the plan anyway.

Even though Jina Wheeler was a trained sharpshooter, they were always cautious about putting one of their own in the line of danger.

Knowing Jina, she'd jump at the chance to prove herself. She always wanted to be involved, regardless of the danger level. She was more than competent, though. The woman spent more time at the shooting range than all the team members combined.

Then again, she had zillions of bull's-eye hits to her credit. Proof that practice did indeed make perfect.

Grabbing the computer, he headed for the sofa. He did more searches on social media, then set it aside. A wave of fatigue washed over him. He doused the lights, removed his utility belt and gun, then stretched out on the too-small sofa.

There was no logical reason for him not to use the perfectly good bed in the second room. Only the impossible to ignore need to stay close to Harper.

He dozed, coming abruptly awake at the sound of movement. After listening for a moment, he relaxed, realizing the sound was coming from her room.

It must be a bummer to have a baby pressing on your bladder, he thought, as he shifted into a more comfortable position.

The next thing he knew the early light of dawn filtered through the windows. He groaned as he rolled off the sofa, his body still sore from the cramped position.

After a quick shower in his bathroom, he donned his uniform, replaced his belt and holster, then padded toward the coffee maker, frowning when he realized they were almost out of coffee. There was only one cup left, aside from the decaf he'd offered to make for Harper.

Nope. Decaf wasn't going to cut it. Not when they were facing a brutal gunrunner in a few hours. With a sigh, he made a call to room service to ask for more. As far as he was concerned, he wasn't giving up this location anytime soon.

He sent a quick text to Brock, making sure his teammate would be at the hotel in a timely manner. Brock agreed to show up by nine.

Hearing movement from Harper's room, he glanced up in time to see her stepping through the doorway. As always, the sight of her stole his breath. Her hair was loose around her shoulders, her green eyes bright. He had the strongest urge to pull her into his arms and kiss her again. One taste had only left him wanting more.

Since when did he find pregnant women attractive?

Since never.

Until Harper.

Man, he was in trouble. Big, big trouble.

"Good morning," she greeted him with a warm smile.

"Good morning." He did his best to mask his thoughts. Professional. He needed to view her as a victim. "Ah, do you want me to make a pot of decaf? That's all we have left until room service shows up with a fresh pot."

"Sure, thanks." She glanced at the sofa cushions that were in disarray with a frown. "You slept on the couch again?"

"Yeah. It's not so bad." He busied himself with making the coffee. "I'd like to get to the precinct early, but we have plenty of time for breakfast."

"It seems like all I'm doing is eating," she said with a frown. "I'm not used to such large meals."

He was worried she wasn't eating enough. Didn't pregnant women burn more calories doing everyday things? He felt certain he'd heard Rhy mention that at one point when his wife was pregnant. And why was he obsessing over it? "Would you rather pick up something along the way?"

"Yeah, maybe." She shifted from one foot to the other. "I'm feeling blah this morning."

"Would you like to cancel the meeting?"

"No!" Her tone didn't leave room for argument. "I'm just tired or something. Maybe the stress is wearing on me."

He wished he could assure her that it would all be over soon, but that wasn't likely. "Sit down, Harper. Enjoy your decaf coffee." He handed her a cup doctored with cream the way she liked, grateful when she sat at the table. "Have you thought about what you'll say to your ex?"

"That's all I've thought about," she admitted. Then she tipped her head to the side. "Are you going to interview him too?"

"Probably." He'd ask as many questions as the ATF

agents would allow. Feldman was in their custody, not his. Although he wished more than once he could get his hands on the guy. Not least of all for hurting Harper.

"Do you think he knows Ellis is dead?"

He shrugged. When he'd discussed the plan with Rhy, the ATF agents had made it clear they hadn't told Feldman anything about Starkey's murder. "I guess that depends on whether he had anything to do with it. He's in protective custody, which means he's not supposed to have access to a phone or a computer. If the ATF agents are keeping a close eye on him, then the news should be a surprise. If not and he somehow got word out to silence the guy . . ." He spread his hands. "Anything is possible."

"Yeah. That's what I think too." She sipped the coffee. "It's difficult to comprehend he could be so callous as to kill his best friend. But obviously, I don't know anything about the real Jake Feldman."

He nodded. "I get that."

"I want to do this, to confront him once and for all." She eyed him over the rim of her cup. "But I'll also be glad when it's over."

Right there with you, he thought with a sigh.

When the room service coffee arrived, he refilled his cup. Then he called Rhy. "I assume it's a go?"

"Yes. Feldman is en route." There was a brief pause before Rhy continued, "He has no idea what the meeting is about. The ATF agents are hoping to gauge his reaction to seeing Harper alive and well."

"Yeah." He glanced at Harper, who appeared lost in thought. "Listen, I'm planning to head over to the precinct early. Brock is meeting us here in about thirty minutes. I'd like some time to talk if you can squeeze me in."

"Not a problem," Rhy assured him. "Let me know when you get here."

"I will. Thanks." He ended the call. "We're a go. Are you sure you don't want breakfast? Brock will be here soon, but we can wait a bit."

Wrinkling her nose, she shook her head. "Not now. Maybe we can pick something up after the meeting. I'm sure my stomach will be settled by then."

He frowned. "Are you due to see your OB doctor soon?"

"Not for another week." She waved a hand dismissively. "I'm fine. Nothing less stress won't cure."

He let it go, knowing Harper would never intentionally allow anything to happen to her baby. If she was concerned, she'd tell him.

Women had babies all the time. Even though they'd been in danger, she hadn't overtaxed herself physically. Jumping the fence had been the worst.

But emotionally, yeah. That came with being framed for murder. And running from constant danger.

His phone buzzed with a text from Brock. *On the road. Will be there in fifteen.*

He thought about that, and answered, *We'll meet you at the side exit.*

Brock sent a quick *Ok* in reply.

"We'll be meeting Brock shortly," he told Harper. "How are your feet?"

"Fine. The blisters are healing nicely." She set her empty cup aside and stood. "I'll use the bathroom quick, then we can go."

Less than five minutes later, she returned to the living area. He held his coat for her. Thankfully, his vest kept him warm enough.

She walked into the hall and turned as if to go to the lobby.

"This way." He caught her hand. "Brock will meet us at the side exit."

"Got it." She didn't pull out of his grasp, her small fingers warm within his.

When they reached the end of the hall, he paused at the door, peering out through the glass to look for Brock. There was no sign of his teammate, or anyone else.

The rental SUV was right where he'd left it.

Five full minutes passed before he saw Brock's SUV. His teammate had taken the time to back in so that Harper could slip directly into the back seat, leaving Steele to slide into the passenger seat.

He opened the door, then used his body as a shield so Harper could get inside. Then he slid into the passenger seat. He glanced at Brock as he slammed his car door. "Let's hit it . . ."

A loud explosion cut him off midsentence. Brock's vehicle jolted wildly from the blast, and his buddy instinctively slammed his foot down on the accelerator, getting them out of there.

Steele twisted in his seat, stunned at seeing the rental SUV parked behind them engulfed in flames.

CHAPTER TWELVE

Her ears were ringing from the blast. Harper noticed Steele and Brock were talking but couldn't hear what they were saying. The vehicle had literally left the pavement from the force of the explosion, but as far as she could tell, their car was still working. Brock was driving away from the City Central Hotel as fast as traffic would allow.

A wave of horror washed over her. If she and Steele had gone to the meeting in the rental vehicle, they'd be dead.

Swallowing hard, she sent up a silent prayer of thanks to God for watching over them. Again. Or maybe still.

She wasn't sure of anything anymore.

She opened her eyes when Brock took a sharp turn.

"Steele?" Even her own voice sounded muffled, as if she had cotton in her ears. Was this hearing loss permanent? "I can't hear you."

Steele twisted in his seat, his expression set in stone. "Are you okay? The baby?"

The words were still muffled, but at least she heard him. She covered her abdomen with her hands, waiting for movement. For a long moment, she didn't feel anything, then the baby shifted in her womb. "I—yes. I think so."

Sirens wailed in the distance, and she was relieved to hear them.

"Where to?" Brock asked. His voice was louder now. Or her hearing was improving. Hopefully the latter. "Still the precinct?"

"No," Steele answered at the same time she said, "Yes."

He turned to scowl at her. "Not happening."

"The blast was meant to keep us from meeting with Jake, right?" She held his gaze. "That means we may learn something important by talking to him."

"No, the blast was meant to kill us," Steele retorted. "It may not be related to the meeting at all."

"But if it is connected to the meeting, Harper's right," Brock said. "There could be some intel to gain from this interview."

She couldn't believe Brock was on her side for once. "It's safe enough at the precinct, isn't it? Plenty of cops around."

"Not necessarily," Steele said harshly. "Last month a cold-blooded killer tried to shoot Elly right outside the rear exit."

She wasn't sure how to respond to that. It would take some nerve to attempt to kill someone at a police station. But she couldn't let fear stop her, not now. "I trust you and Brock to keep me safe."

"Yeah," Steele drawled. "Because we're doing such a bang-up job of that."

"Hey, we're not hurt," Brock pointed out. "We must be doing something right."

"Sheer luck." Steele shook his head. "If we had driven ourselves to the precinct in the rental SUV . . ."

"We didn't," she quickly interjected. "And it's not luck, God watching over us." She leaned forward as much as her seat belt would allow. "Please head for the precinct. I think this interview could be important."

Steele sat quietly for a long moment. "Fine." He was obviously not happy about the plan. "But I'm calling Joe." He pulled the phone from his pocket. "I want him and other members of the team to be there waiting for us to arrive. I don't like the way our hotel was found."

That she could agree with. She eyed his phone. "Do you think we were tracked to the hotel through your phone?"

He glanced at her in surprise. "I would say yes, except we've been at the City Central Hotel for more than thirty-six hours. Why wait until now to strike?"

"How else, then?" She pressed. The memory of how Bryon Perkins smirked at her upon finding the gun in her dresser flashed in her mind. "Maybe one or both of the ATF agents are involved."

"Anything is possible, and I'm willing to ditch my phone," Steele agreed. "But don't forget you called your boss and logged into work."

"What?" Brock's eyes were wide with surprise as he met her gaze in the rearview. "Why would you do something like that?" He acted as if she'd committed some huge transgression. What else was she supposed to do all day? Twiddle her thumbs?

"I'm burning vacation time I can't afford to lose. I was hoping to save more time for after I deliver my baby." She shook her head, wishing they could understand how important it was for her to keep her job. "There's no way Gibson and Roberts are involved. The tracking source has to be your phone, Steele."

"Maybe." He called Joe to make the arrangements, then

surprised her by lowering the window and tossing the device out. It bounced off the concrete pavement once, then a second time, shattering into pieces.

"I'll pick up new phones later," Brock said after a moment of silence. "For both of us."

Steele nodded but didn't say anything more. She sat back in her seat, doing her best to shake off the impending feeling of doom. They were safe, the explosion hadn't hurt them. But if the bomb had been planted just to prevent her from speaking with Jake, she couldn't help feeling more nervous than ever about confronting her ex-husband.

Her idea, remember? She took slow deep breaths to lower her stress level. She needed to remain calm for her baby's sake. No matter what happened during the meeting, Steele and Brock would protect her. No question about that. Words couldn't hurt her.

Well, they might wound her on an emotional level, but she would do her best to ignore whatever scathing comments Jake threw her way. He was the one who'd been arrested and tossed in jail.

And the one who'd agreed to testify against Tommy Grotto to save his own skin.

"You're sure you're, okay?" Steele frowned, concern darkening his blue eyes.

"Yes." As okay as she could be considering the circumstances. There was a part of her that wanted to raise her fist at God, asking why he was punishing her like this. Hadn't she paid enough for her bad decision to marry Jake?

"We're here," Brock said. "Looks like Joe and Raelyn are outside waiting for us."

She noticed the two cops dressed in full tactical gear standing like sentries on either side of the door. She sincerely hoped there wasn't any danger nearby. When

Brock rolled up alongside the doorway, Joe's eyes widened in shock.

"Wow, looks like you drove past a sand blaster." He shook his head and winced. "Most of the paint is gone along the back of the SUV. That's going to cost a pretty penny to fix."

"At least we're alive to talk about it," Brock shot back. "Thankfully, I paid for the extra insurance."

"Smart move." Joe stepped forward to open her door.

"Been there, done that," Brock said half under his breath. "Standard operating procedure from now on."

She unbuckled her seat belt and scooted over to get out of the car. Joe stayed on one side, with Raelyn coming up to stand at the other. If the situation wasn't so dire, she'd joke about being treated like a movie star. Steele joined them, taking up a position behind her as they made their way inside.

"Have a seat over here." Steele gestured toward a desk chair in a cubicle. "I need to speak with Rhy."

She shrugged, dropping into the empty seat. Glancing around, she wondered if Jake was here in one of the interview rooms or if the ATF agents assigned to protect him were still on the road.

Raelyn hovered nearby. "Can I get you anything? Water? Coffee?"

"Water would be nice." She managed a smile.

"Coming up." Raelyn disappeared into a room off to the side, which she assumed was some sort of break room.

They'd originally left the hotel with plenty of time, but she'd noticed Brock took a major detour after leaving the scene of the explosion. He strode toward her cubicle. "Where's Steele?"

"He wanted to talk to Rhy. Is Jake here yet?"

"They're only ten minutes out." Brock shrugged. "They're bringing him in through the back too. Come with me, we're going to have you wait in Rhy's office until they're settled in the conference room."

"Okay." Raelyn joined them, handing Harper a bottle of water. She followed Brock to Rhy's office.

"I'm concerned about the ATF—" Steele abruptly stopped talking when he noticed they were all behind him. "What's going on?"

"It's better if Harper sits here until Jake and the ATF agents are settled in the conference room," Brock explained. He shot a glance at Rhy. "They'll be here in ten. You okay with that?"

"Sure, come in, Harper." Steele stepped aside so she could take the chair.

"Thanks." She wasn't sure all this subterfuge was necessary, but considering the recent explosion, she understood they weren't taking any chances. She sipped her water, willing her stomach to settle. It was a good thing they'd skipped breakfast.

"We'll check all options," Rhy said, apparently responding to Steele's comment. "Michaels is on board."

Steele nodded, his expression still set in a scowl.

An uncomfortable silence fell between them. Finally, Brock said, "Steele ditched his phone. I'm going to head out to get replacements."

"Take a squad," Rhy advised. "Your damaged SUV will stand out like a sore thumb."

"Will do." Brock turned and left.

A few minutes later, Rhy's phone rang. He picked up the receiver. "Finnegan." He looked thoughtful as he listened, then said, "Okay, we'll bring her in shortly."

Her stomach knotted. "He's here?"

"Yes." Rhy smiled reassuringly. "Steele and Raelyn will be with you the entire time."

"Okay." She stood. Raelyn led the way, with Steele staying close behind her.

It was the same interview room she'd been in before. Raelyn opened the door and crossed the threshold. Then she gestured for Harper to come in. Her gaze was focused on Jake, the man she hadn't seen in over seven months, except on TV during his arrest.

He smirked, then his jaw dropped as his gaze focused on her belly. The shock was too real to be faked.

Jake had not known she was pregnant with their child.

WELL, *well, well,* Steele thought. Feldman hadn't known about Harper's pregnancy. Maybe the guy wasn't communicating with anyone to coordinate these attacks.

"Why are you trying to kill me?" Harper's blunt question caught them all off guard.

"I'm not." Jake scowled. "Why didn't you tell me you were knocked up?"

"You didn't arrange for me to be kidnapped outside the law office where I work?" Harper persisted, ignoring his question. "Or hire someone to shoot me?"

"What is this?" Jake demanded, raking his gaze around the room. "What's she talking about?"

To Steele's eye, Feldman's surprise appeared real. He hadn't known about the baby or the abduction attempt or the shootings.

"Your ex-wife is in grave danger," Steele said. "Seems someone from within your organization wants to kill her. Any idea why?"

"That's ridiculous," Jake snapped. "She doesn't know anything."

"Clearly, someone believes she does," Steele drawled. "Hence the recent attacks."

Jake appeared nervous. "Look, I don't have any control over Grotto and Brooks. If they're going after her, it's nothing to do with me."

"Be serious," one of the ATF agents said. "Obviously, an attack against your ex-wife is all about you."

Jake's wrists were cuffed to the table, but he turned his hands palms up. "I don't know anything about that! How could I? You've kept me under lock and key for months now."

Again, he came across as believable. Yet Steele wasn't convinced. "What information do you have on Grotto and Brooks? We need to find them ASAP."

"I don't know where they are," Feldman protested. "I gave the ATF the names of their contacts in Chicago and Detroit."

"You must know where they would be hiding out," Harper said. She leaned forward. "Did you know they brutally killed Ellis? Shot him execution style in the back of his head?"

The color drained from Jake's face. "When?"

"Tell us what you know." Steele stepped closer to the table, lightly resting his hand on Harper's shoulder. He'd wanted to give her a chance to confront her ex, but giving the guy information on an active investigation wasn't part of the plan.

Feldman glanced from one ATF agent to the other. Finally, he said, "Grotto had a place in the Third Ward. I don't know if he's still using it, though."

"Where in the Third Ward?" Steele demanded.

Feldman gave him an address. The ATF agent to Feldman's right pulled out his phone and sent a message, likely to either Perkins or Banner. "That wasn't so hard, was it?" the ATF agent asked.

Feldman hunched his shoulders. "You guys gotta promise to keep me safe."

"Your ex-wife deserves the same courtesy," Steele said. "What about an address for Waylon Brooks?"

"I already gave them that," Feldman protested.

One ATF agent nodded. "Perkins checked it out. No sign of the guy."

"Well, let's hope he doesn't end up like Starkey," Steele muttered. "Anything else?"

"No." Jake stared down at the table as if he couldn't bear to meet Harper's gaze. "I've given you everything I know."

Bringing the interview to an end, Steele escorted Harper back out to Rhy's office. "Stay here until they take Feldman outside."

She was unusually subdued. He dropped to one knee beside her. "You don't look happy, Harper. I warned you that confronting your ex wouldn't be pleasant."

"It never occurred to me that he hadn't heard about my pregnancy." Her voice was so low it was difficult to hear. "I—should have thought this through."

He wasn't sure what to say. "I'm sure once he testifies against Grotto, he'll be relocated to the other side of the country."

"But he'll be free, right?" She lifted her dark-green eyes to his. "There would be nothing holding him back from coming to find me. To try to see his son or daughter."

"Do you have reason to believe he'd want the child?"

"No. I mean, I don't think so." She gnawed on her lower lip. "But I can't bear the thought of him coming to find me."

Was she saying she wanted to be placed in witness protection too? Oddly that idea was repugnant. He didn't want Harper to leave the city, moving to a new location to start over.

Then he reminded himself he shouldn't be selfish. "If you want to be set up with a new identity, we can make those arrangements."

"No, I don't want to leave here, this is my home. I've made friends in church. But . . ." She shrugged. "I don't know what to do. I was such a fool to insist on confronting Jake."

He hesitated, then said, "You don't have to decide anything now, Harper."

She nodded and tucked a strand of her long blond hair behind her ear. "What's next?"

"We need to find a new place to stay." He'd been about to ask Rhy about a safe house when they'd interrupted his meeting with the captain. He wanted a place that was well under the radar of even the ATF agents assigned to the case.

"Another hotel?" Harper asked.

He inwardly sighed. "For now."

"What about the computer we had to leave behind?" Harper asked. "Can we go back to get it? I'd like to be able to get a little more work done."

"No way." His tone was sharper than he'd intended. "I don't think you should log into work again anyway. We don't know for sure how we were found."

"It makes no sense that my boss would be involved," she insisted. "He's a very successful lawyer. And if he wanted me to be taken, why not wait until I was up in the office?"

She had a point. "What about one of his clients?"

"What reason would a client have to come after me?" She rubbed her temple. "You don't seem to get how important it is for me to have time off after my baby is born."

"I do understand." He reached for her hand. "I got a text from Brock. He'll be here soon. We can probably grab one of the computers here to use for a while."

"Okay."

He squeezed her hand and stood. When he'd glimpsed the spreadsheet over her shoulder, he'd noticed many billable hours assigned to Neil Otterson. He knew Otterson had been arrested for killing two young Hispanic men in a so-called attempted carjacking. But maybe there was more to the guy than they knew.

"Make yourself at home," Rhy said with a smile when he returned to his office.

"We did, thanks. Hey, will you give me Brady's number?" He reached for his boss's phone. "I want to run something past him."

"Sure." Rhy rattled off the number. It didn't take long for Rhy's brother Brady Finnegan to answer. "What's up, Rhy?"

"Oh, sorry, it's Steele using Rhy's phone. I was wondering if you could search on a guy using the FBI database."

"Got a name?" Steele could hear fingers tapping on a keyboard in the background.

"Neil Otterson. I don't have a date of birth, but he's been charged with first-degree murder for killing two young Hispanic men during a carjacking. It's on the Wisconsin Circuit case website."

"Alleged carjacking?" Brady echoed in surprise. "Typically, those types of scenarios don't result in a charge of first-

degree murder. Maybe reckless homicide, but not premedi-
tated murder."

"Yeah, but it sounds like there was no evidence of an
attempted carjacking, and the two guys weren't armed. I'm
not privy to all the details on the case," he hastened to add.
"I'm curious if there's anything else you can dig up on the
guy."

"Okay, I'll see what I can find," Brady agreed.

"One more thing." He glanced at his boss, then decided
there was no point in beating around the bush. "Do you
have any intel on two ATF agents by the name of Bryon
Perkins or Steve Banner?"

"You mean, like are they on the take?" Brady asked in
surprise.

"Yeah." He avoided Rhy's gaze. "I've been protecting a
witness for the past few days, and we keep getting found. I
don't like thinking they're dirty, but I don't know these ATF
guys very well either. This case has been a struggle from the
beginning, and it's not getting any better."

"There's nothing on our radar that I'm aware of. Hang
on a minute." Based on the music in his ear, Brady put him
on hold.

"You really think the feds wouldn't have told us if there
was something sketchy about those guys?" Rhy asked.

"I had to ask." He didn't like sounding defensive. "The
rental car exploded, nearly taking us with it. Don't you
think it's better that we cover all bases?"

"Yes, but if Brady had heard something about the ATF
being sketchy, he'd call me." Rhy looked exasperated. "I'm
his brother. He's not going to hold back on important intel
that could impact the safety of my team."

It was hard to argue Rhy's point. A moment later, Brady
came back on the call. "I checked with Marc Callahan and

our DEA agent liaison, Doug Bridges. No one is aware of concerns around a bad ATF agent."

"Okay, thanks for checking." He refused to feel guilty for asking the question. Moving forward, he couldn't afford to trust anyone. "Will you also let me know about Otterson? I'd like to make sure he's not a possible suspect in this."

"Yeah, I'll get in touch if I learn anything." Brady paused, then asked, "What's your phone number?"

"Ah, hang on." Brock strode toward the office carrying a bag. Steele waved him over, reached into the bag, and pulled out one of the disposable phones. He gave the number to Brady. "Thanks again."

"No problem. I'll be in touch." Brady disconnected from the call.

"We may as well get these powered up," Brock said. "It's better to have a working phone while we're out on the road."

Rhy drummed his fingers on the desk. "What's your next move?"

Good question. Too bad he didn't have an equally good answer. "We could set a trap, using a female officer to pretend to be Harper."

"Like Jina?" Rhy frowned. "Maybe, but I don't like putting my cops in harm's way."

"I know, I don't either. What about allowing us to use that safe house, the one with bulletproof glass?"

"Last I checked, it's currently in use," Rhy said. "I have Harper on the list, though."

He scowled. "She should take priority."

Rhy arched a brow. "I can't move one witness out to make room for another just because she's pregnant."

"It's okay, I understand," Harper spoke up. "And I don't think you should use Jina to impersonate me either."

"We'll talk about that," Rhy hedged. Then he turned his

gaze back to his. "Why don't you head to the Timberland Falls Suites? We've used it before. And it's nicer than City Central."

Timberland Falls was roughly eighteen miles from the precinct. "It's a little far."

"Far enough that no one should find you there." Rhy reached for the phone. "I'll make the arrangements."

It was on the tip of his tongue to remind his boss that he'd made the arrangements for the City Central suite too. Then again, they had been safe until this morning.

He really wished he knew how they'd been found.

The meeting with Feldman had been a bust. Sure, he'd given them the location of Grotto's Third Ward hideout, but they likely would have gotten that information from him regardless of Harper being there. And there was also the fact that Feldman should have given them that information long before today.

He kicked himself for allowing her to sway him into agreeing to the interview. This was what happened when you let a victim get too close. He was making the same mistake Joe had with Elly.

Maybe having Harper go into witness protection would be the best option for her.

Rhy's phone rang. His boss answered it, then looked up at Steele. "Brady's returning your call. I'll put him on speaker."

"Hey, Brady, that was quick."

"Yeah, well, I was curious about the case too. The truth is that Otterson is a suspect related to the murder of a federal agent two years ago. The problem is there's no evidence linking him to the guy's death."

"And that relates to his current charges, how?" he asked.

"I think the feds pressured the DA's office to throw

serious charges at him to buy time to dig into the case further. My take? They think the slaying of the two kids is related to other illegal activity."

He met Harper's shocked gaze. Illegal activity?

Like buying and selling guns?

CHAPTER THIRTEEN

Goose bumps rose along her skin. Harper hadn't taken Steele's concerns about Neil Otterson seriously, but maybe there was a connection. It still didn't make sense that the guy would come after her, though. She was only an administrative assistant for Trent Gibson. Not even a paralegal, something she'd once planned to return to school for until learning she was pregnant. Yes, she had access to sensitive files, but if Neil Otterson really thought she'd violated his privacy, he'd have her fired.

Not try to kidnap and kill her.

Yet for the first time, she felt apprehensive about the possibility of Trent prevailing in court, getting Neil Otterson acquitted and allowing the guy to go free.

"Thanks, Brady." She glanced up as Steele disconnected from the call. She frowned, realizing she'd missed the tail end of the phone call between Steele and Brady.

"That's interesting," Rhy mused.

"Yeah." Steele looked thoughtful for a long moment. "I'll see if there's anything else I can dig up on the two Hispanic victims."

"Sounds like a plan. I'll talk to Michaels and Jina about possibly drawing the shooter out too." Rhy narrowed his gaze. "No promises, though."

"I understand." Steele glanced at her. "Are you ready to get out of here?"

She nodded and rose to her feet. Steele placed his hand beneath her elbow to help steady her. She wanted to reiterate that having Jina pretending to be her was a bad idea but decided to keep quiet. It sounded as if Rhy wasn't enthused about the plan anyway.

"Lead the way, Brock," Steele said. "We'll go out the same way we came in."

She remained silent as they wove their way through the cubicles toward the rear exit. The more she thought about it, she couldn't link the attacks against her to Neil Otterson.

The explosion of their rental SUV had badly shaken her. She couldn't become paralyzed by fear. Neil Otterson was a client of Gibson and Roberts, not a threat.

Brock opened the door and glanced around for a long moment before stepping outside. She followed his lead, keeping herself positioned behind him as he led the way to the vehicle. She slid into the back, leaving the two men to sit in the front.

"Was it worth it?" Brock's question had her lifting her gaze to the rearview mirror. "Did you get what you wanted out of the interview with your ex-husband?"

"No." She looked away, wishing she hadn't been so eager to face off with Jake. The frank surprise in his gaze when he realized she was pregnant replayed in her brain. "I guess Steele was right all along. Nothing good came from this meeting."

Another long uncomfortable silence fell between them.

She noticed the series of glances Brock and Steele exchanged but ignored them.

She had no one to blame for her foolishness but herself. She prayed Jake wouldn't make trouble for her once the trial was over and he was placed in witness protection.

And if he did? Her stomach knotted painfully. She'd have to find a way to disappear herself. How she'd manage to do that with a newborn baby, she had no clue. She didn't have money and wasn't sure how she'd get a decent job without a reference from Trent Gibson.

How much time did she have before she had to worry about Jake? Three months? Six months? Maybe a year at the most.

"Are you hungry?" Steele's voice broke into her thoughts. "We didn't eat breakfast. I don't think it's smart to miss meals."

Her stomach churned, but that could be in part due to hunger. "That's fine."

"I'll hit a fast-food place near Timberland Falls," Brock offered.

"Whatever works." She wasn't in a position to be picky. She grimaced, wishing she hadn't been forced to leave her toiletries behind.

A minor inconvenience, she reminded herself sternly. Staying alive was all that mattered.

True to his word, Brock found a drive-through restaurant. The scent of their egg sandwiches smelled good, stirring her appetite. No doubt God's way of making sure she ate enough for her baby to thrive.

Five minutes later, they were back on the road. When he pulled into the parking lot of the Timberland Falls Suites, she couldn't help being impressed. There was a layer of fresh snow covering the trees behind the hotel, and the building looked upscale. It was pretty, like something out of a movie.

Brock parked in front of the main entrance. Steele opened her door, then escorted her inside, bringing their food with him.

The lobby of the hotel was huge, and there was a stone fireplace off to one side. The fire was lit, sending waves of heat toward her. She almost wished she could just sit in front of the fire for the rest of the day but followed Steele and Brock as they headed to their room.

Brock set the computer aside as Steele unpacked their meal. She took off her coat, pulled out the vitamins, then dropped into the closest chair. Steele must have noticed the bottle because he turned to the sink to pour her a glass of water.

"Thanks." She reached for her breakfast sandwich before remembering to pray. Bowing her head, she said, "Dear Lord Jesus, we are blessed to have this food You've provided for us. We are grateful for Your love and protection. Amen."

"Amen," Steele and Brock added. She was used to Steele praying, but Brock usually remained silent.

"Who pays for all this?" She waved a hand at the large suite. "I'm feeling guilty over the amount of money we're going through."

"Rhy booked it." Steele shrugged. "I expect he'll get reimbursed by the department."

Brock looked a little surprised but didn't respond. She wondered if Steele had only said that to make her feel better.

She had to force herself to eat. She wanted to believe God was watching over them, but it wasn't easy.

"I'd like to call my boss," she said, breaking the silence.

"You're not working from the hotel, end of story," Steele said curtly.

She stared at him, reining in her own temper. "I understand your concern, but I only said I needed to talk to my boss. Not log onto the computer system."

"I still don't like it," Steele said, softening his tone.

"Yeah, well, I need to talk to him. He thinks I'll be working. He needs to know the plan has changed."

"He'll figure that out when you don't do any work," Steele said.

"These attacks are most likely related to my ex-husband." She kept her voice mild. "It's a simple, short phone call."

Brock watched the interchange between them without interrupting.

"Fine." Steele reluctantly agreed. "But then we're going to get rid of your phone. That way, it can't be tracked."

Since she'd insinuated his phone had been the source of their being found at City Central, she couldn't very well argue. Her breakfast sandwich sat like a lump in her stomach. She ate most of it, then pushed it away.

She stood and fished her phone from Steele's coat pocket. She made the call to Trent, who didn't answer. She left a very brief message about not being able to work, then disconnected. She tossed the phone onto the table so that it slid to Steele. "Take it. Apparently, I won't need it."

"Thanks." He took the phone, powered it down, then stomped on it with his heel.

Her stomach cramped, and she turned away to head to the closest bedroom. She sat on the edge of the bed, smoothing her palms over her belly, waiting for it to pass. Thankfully, after a few minutes, she felt better.

Yet she sensed the physical discomfort was a warning.

All this stress wasn't good for her or the baby. She needed to find some level of peace.

She propped herself up against the headboard, closed her eyes, and prayed. She didn't know exactly what to say but silently repeated the few prayers she could remember from church.

"Harper?" She opened her eyes to find Steele hovering in the doorway. "Is everything okay?"

She was about to nod, then hesitated. "Honestly, I'm not sure. I had some cramping earlier. It's better now, but I'm a little worried."

Concern furrowed his brow as he stepped into the room. "Should we go to the hospital?"

"Not yet, but if it continues, then yes. I don't want to take a chance on something bad happening."

"You say the word, and we'll go." He sat on the edge of the bed. "I'm sorry things didn't turn out as well as you'd hoped today."

"You told me not to do it." With a grimace, she realized she sounded petulant. "We learned Jake isn't paying someone to do attack me. He hadn't even known about the baby. If he had been in contact with someone outside of the safe house, he'd have known about my condition. And he did give you an address."

"Yeah, but Raelyn called to say the place was empty." Steele's tone indicated he thought Jake had led them astray on purpose. "The crime scene techs are going over it anyway, just in case."

She feared this nightmare would never end. On the heels of that thought came another strong cramp.

Or was it a contraction? Fear rose like a lump in the back of her throat.

"Harper?" Steele reached over to cover her hand with his. "Is this another cramp?"

"Yes." She held his gaze. "I think we better go in."

"Right away." He shot off the bed and called to Brock. "I need you to drive the SUV to the lobby entrance."

"What's going on?" Brock asked.

"Harper needs to get checked out at the hospital. Hurry."

She spent a moment smoothing her hands over her belly, then slowly swung her legs over the edge of the bed. Maybe this wasn't anything to panic about. She'd read parts of the pregnancy book she'd gotten from the library and remembered something about Braxton Hicks contractions. She didn't remember if they started within the seventh month of pregnancy, though. She wished she'd brought the book with her.

Brock covered the distance between the hotel and Trinity Medical Center in record time. The nurse at the front desk of the emergency department took her immediately back to a room. Steele stayed at her side.

The nurse glanced at him warily. "Ms. Crane, would you like your significant other to say in the room while you change into a hospital gown?"

"No, he's not . . ." She hesitated, unsure what to say. "Steele, will you please wait outside?"

"Of course." He flashed a reassuring smile, then stepped back into the hall.

By the time she'd changed, the cramp had subsided. The nurse asked her dozens of questions about her pregnancy and her recent health history. A kind female physician joined them.

"I'm Dr. Faye Finnegan," she introduced herself.

"Related to Rhy Finnegan?" Harper asked.

The physician laughed. "Yes, I'm married to Colin. But let's talk about what you're going through, shall we?"

Harper answered more questions as Dr. Finnegan listened to the baby's heartbeat. Finally, she said, "I'm going to ask one of the OB specialists to come talk to you. From what I can tell, your baby is fine." Faye searched her gaze. "I noticed the officer outside your door. I suspect you're undergoing a bit of stress."

She let out a weary laugh. "Yeah, you could say that."

"I know you're aware that's not good for you or your baby." Her gaze held compassion. "I also know you're doing your best. I'm sure this situation is outside your control. We'll see what the OB has to say, but my best advice is to practice relaxation techniques."

"I've been doing deep-breathing techniques but will try harder." She liked Faye Finnegan. "Thanks for reassuring me."

"The OB should be down shortly." Faye smiled again, then moved to the door. "Take care, Harper."

"Thanks, you too." Harper expected Steele to come in, but he didn't. Maybe he'd decided to grab some coffee. Spying the phone on the bedside table, she reached over and drew it closer.

Without giving herself time to think, she lifted the receiver and punched in Trent Gibson's number. This time, he answered after three rings. "Gibson and Roberts."

"Trent, it's Harper." Now that she had him on the line, she wasn't sure how much to tell him. She decided to start with the topic foremost on her mind. "Trent, I'm in the hospital. I've been having some abdominal cramping. The doctor seems to think I'll be fine, but I just wanted you to know."

"I'm sorry to hear that." Genuine concern laced his tone. "What can I do?"

"Nothing, really, except I don't think I'll be able to work from home for a little while." She was deliberately vague about the timing. "I'm really sorry about that, I know I'm burning vacation time I can't afford to lose."

"You just take care of yourself," he said firmly. "You'll get six weeks paid sick leave regardless. Whatever vacation time you've accrued can be tacked on to extend your leave. And if you need an additional day or two to work from home, that can be arranged too."

"Really?" Relief washed over her. "I appreciate that so much, Trent. Thanks."

"You're welcome. Take care, Harper." He didn't linger but ended the call. As she replaced the phone, she let out a sigh.

Trent wasn't involved in this. She refused to believe he would risk her life or that of her baby.

Steele and Brock and the others were on the wrong track. And maybe she needed to stay out of it. Getting wrapped up in the case to the point of insisting on meeting with Jake had not been good for her or the baby.

From this point onward, she was going to stay focused on her own health and well-being.

Not the case.

STEELE HAD OVERHEARD Harper's side of the phone call with her boss. At first, he was upset about her using the hospital phone to call him, then he realized it was probably safer for her in the long run.

And he'd felt bad when she'd voiced her concern over

her maternity leave. Obviously, stress wasn't good for her. Yet she'd been worrying about her time off and keeping her job.

The way they'd been investigating Neil Otterson likely hadn't helped. And he had to take responsibility for that. Somehow, the line between his being a cop and Harper a victim had gotten blurred.

To the point he'd been sharing too much information with her.

No more, he silently lectured himself.

He knew they were still waiting for the OB doctor to examine her. He peeked in on Harper to find her lying still with her eyes closed. Deciding to let her rest, he joined Brock in the waiting room.

"She okay?" Brock asked. Despite his original distrust of Harper, Brock seemed to have come around to believing her.

"Yeah, but we need to find a way to limit her stress."

Brock arched a brow. "No easy task."

"Tell me about it." He scrubbed his hands over his face. "What have you been doing while waiting?"

"I've been texting with Rhy, they have a lead on the case. And it may intersect with our case."

He straightened, his heart thumping with anticipation. "What lead?"

"You're not going to believe this, but that gun Otterson used to shoot the two young men who allegedly tried to rob him matches the slug found in the dead federal agent."

"No way," Steele protested. "That should have been enough to arrest him on federal charges."

"Yep. Apparently, Otterson had given the cops a receipt for the gun purchase, claiming he didn't have the gun two years ago and that someone else must have used it to commit the crime, but they aren't buying it. Not when they have a definitive match."

"And they just found that ballistics match now?" Steele asked incredulously.

"Yeah, that's the downside. Apparently, there was a mix-up at the lab. Some paperwork got misfiled, either by accident or on purpose." Brock shrugged. "The bottom line is that there's a new federal warrant out for Neil Otterson's arrest."

"That's good news," Steele agreed. Although he didn't like hearing about sloppy police work. Or a possible mole in the lab. This was why many people didn't trust the police. These kinds of errors shouldn't happen. "Although I don't know that it's going to help the case of the dead agent as much as they hope it will. Trent Gibson, Otterson's defense lawyer, is going to have a field day about the mix-up at the lab. They're going to claim that the reason the match was misfiled or misplaced was because they're framing Otterson for the crime."

"I hear you," Brock agreed. "It's not great for the feds, and Rhy is not at all happy about it either. However, I'm not going to complain about the feds putting Otterson behind bars for a while. This time, because he's being accused of murdering a federal agent, he will not be granted bail. Sitting behind bars for the next few months might be enough to convince Otterson to make a deal."

"Maybe." As he thought about it more, he wondered if having Otterson arrested on federal capital murder charges would impact Trent Gibson's case. The feds often pulled rank over local legal proceedings. He didn't anticipate this would be any different.

Would Trent Gibson make more money as a result of these new charges? Or would Otterson cut him loose and find another attorney? It wouldn't surprise him if Otterson wanted to start over, yet that would also take lots of cash. From the glimpse he'd gotten over Harper's shoulder, Otterson had already paid Gibson more than twice a cop's annual salary.

Normally, he couldn't care less what happened to a defense attorney. He wasn't fond of lawyers who were paid big bucks to keep criminals out of jail. But Trent Gibson was Harper's employer.

And he cared deeply for her. His heart must have decided it was time to move on from Monique. All he could think about was Harper. He couldn't stand the idea that she could lose her job. That she might be forced to start over someplace new this far along in her pregnancy.

Yeah, he cared far more than was good for him. Which was why he'd blurred the line between them. And that idiotic move had contributed to her being here in the hospital.

He blew out a heavy sigh and tried not to think about Harper's role within the law office. Gibson had other clients. She'd be fine.

"Any update from Raelyn on the address Feldman gave us?" Steele asked.

Brock shook his head. "Not yet. They have found some fingerprints, so it's possible they'll match Tommy Grotto. But that alone won't help us find him."

"I'm not sure who is masterminding these attempts on Harper," he confided. "It's either Neil Otterson or Tommy Grotto."

"Or both," Brock said. "I know, I've been going over the possible scenarios too."

"We don't have proof Otterson is involved in selling guns." Steele frowned. "But there's just something about the fact that he killed two young men that is nagging at me."

"We know Tommy Grotto is involved with gunrunning," Brock mused. "But he and Waylon Brooks are in the wind."

The case was maddening. He checked his watch, then stood. "I'm going to check on Harper again. See if the OB has examined her yet."

"Yeah, okay." He had turned away, when Brock said, "You're in pretty deep water there, Steele."

He turned to Brock, knowing exactly what he meant. "I know. I didn't mean to let you and the rest of the team down. I never should have agreed to let her meet with Feldman."

"See, that's exactly what I'm talking about." Brock stood so they were face-to-face. "I think it's good that she met with him. We needed to know for sure if she was involved or not. You're thinking like a concerned boyfriend, not a cop."

He winced. "Yeah, okay. I'll do better from this point on."

"Maybe we should switch things up," Brock suggested. "Have Raelyn or Grayson stay with Harper for a while."

Every cell in his body rejected that idea. But he could tell Brock was pushing his buttons on purpose. "I'm fine with a staffing change." He wasn't but tried to hide his true feelings. "However, I don't want to add more stress to Harper. The doc pretty much told her stress was causing her symptoms. I'm all for maintaining a professional distance, as long as it doesn't impact her unborn child."

Brock stared at him for a long moment. "Okay, we'll discuss this further with Rhy later."

He nodded in agreement and turned to head back to Harper's room. He had to be let back by a security guard, as the hospital had tightened their security measures after a gunman had gotten inside and dressed like one of the staff doctors last month.

Striding to Harper's room, he could hear voices inside. He hung around outside the room to give her privacy.

A moment later, a doc who appeared to be in his midfifties emerged. Steele poked his head around the doorway. "Harper?"

"Come in." She smiled at him. "Dr. Webb has assured me everything is fine."

"That's great news." He couldn't stop himself from reaching for her hand. It was obvious Harper needed a friend. "How much longer are they going to keep you?"

"It sounds like I'll be discharged soon." She clung to his hand for a moment. "Thanks for bringing me in, Steele. I feel so much better now that I've spoken to the doctor."

"Of course, Harper. Anytime." He had trouble looking away from her pretty green eyes.

"Would you help me stand up?"

"Sure." He gently pulled her hand so that she was sitting upright on the edge of the bed. The oversized hospital gown fell off one shoulder, so he quickly pulled the fabric back into place.

"They gave me a full liter of IV fluids." Her cheeks went pink with embarrassment. "I need to use the restroom."

He escorted her to the restroom, then waited for her to emerge.

"Much better." She smiled. "It's the little things."

"I can only imagine." She leaned against him for a moment. When she glanced up, he couldn't seem to tear his gaze from her mouth.

Brock's lecture and even his own determination to stay

detached fled from his mind. He lowered his head, capturing her mouth with his.

Kissing Harper was akin to playing with fire. Yet he couldn't bring himself to care if he got burned. He pulled her closer, angling his head to deepen their kiss.

"Steele." Brock's sharp tone was like a kick in the behind. He broke off the kiss, glancing guiltily at his teammate. The accusation in Brock's eyes made him wince.

"I just got a call from Rhy." Brock glanced at Harper, then back at him. "The feds went to Gibson's office to let the lawyer know about the arrest warrant for Otterson." He paused, then added, "They found Gibson lying on the floor of his office with a head wound."

Gibson was attacked? By Otterson? Or someone else?

He glanced at Harper, seeing the shock in her expression. He had a bad feeling their case had just intersected with the one the feds were working on.

And he did not think that was good for any of them.

Especially Harper.

CHAPTER FOURTEEN

"Is Trent alive?" Harper pushed the question through her tight throat. The family photo of his wife and two young sons flashed in her mind. He had a young family, and she could only imagine what they were going through.

"Yes, he's being transported here, to Trinity Medical Center." Brock frowned. "We need to get you out of here ASAP. I think it's entirely possible the attacks against you are linked to the case against Otterson."

"Agree. Get dressed, Harper." Steele's grim expression mirrored Brock's. "We're leaving."

She wanted to protest that she hadn't been officially discharged but held her tongue. The kind OB doc had indicated she could go home. She'd been reassured her baby was doing well after Dr. Webb had examined her. She scooped her clothes off the chair, then ducked into the bathroom to change.

Who had assaulted Trent? Neil Otterson? But if so, why? It didn't make sense to take out your own defense lawyer.

Unless Otterson's plan was to get rid of the guy so he

wouldn't have to pay his bill. But she knew Neil Otterson had already given Trent a sizable retainer. That was money he'd never get back. And what about that double billing she'd found? Was that part of this?

None of this made any sense.

Especially not the part where Jake's gunrunning operation was somehow linked to Neil Otterson.

Neil was in his midforties by her estimation. Her ex-husband had just turned thirty. Neil had killed two Hispanic men in an apparent carjacking. While Jake had been buying and selling guns, working with sources in Detroit and Chicago. How were they connected?

The troubled thoughts made her head hurt, and she took several deep calming breaths, the warning from Dr. Faye Finnegan about stress not being good for her or the baby echoing in her mind. There was so much she couldn't control, but she could practice stress-relieving techniques, the way Faye had suggested.

Still, she was worried about her boss. Not just because she needed the job at Gibson and Roberts. She cared about Trent. He'd been supportive of her, despite her ex-husband's arrest. Almost treating her like a daughter.

Now he'd been hurt. And she still didn't know who wanted her dead.

Her church pastor would tell her to trust in God's plan. And she was trying to do that. Even if she didn't understand why God's plan meant she and her unborn child needed to be in danger. Then a thought occurred to her. Something the church pastor had said. Life's challenges are often meant to bring a person closer to God.

Feeling calmer, she emerged from the bathroom to find Steele and Brock chatting with Dr. Faye Finnegan.

Faye's sympathetic gaze swung to her. "I've written

your discharge order, Harper. Just remember what I said, okay?"

"I will." She managed a lopsided smile. "No stress."

Steele winced, and even Brock looked guilty. It wasn't as if the danger surrounding her was their fault.

But the end result was still the same.

"Let's go." Steele held up her coat for her. "Brock, will you get the car positioned near the entrance?"

"Yeah." He turned to leave.

"Harper?" Her nurse entered the room with paperwork. "These are your discharge instructions. The providers are requesting you call back or come in to be seen if your condition changes."

"Thanks. I will." She folded the papers and stuffed them into her pocket. "Can we wait long enough to see how Trent is doing?"

"I'm afraid not." Steele urged her forward. "We don't know who attacked your boss or why. It's possible that same person could anticipate he'd be brought here and show up in the emergency department."

To finish the job. Steele hadn't said the words, but they still reverberated through her mind.

He escorted her from the room and through the double doorways leading to the waiting room. The place was half full, but many of the patients waiting to be seen looked far worse than she did. It was probably a good thing she was being discharged so quickly.

Steele hovered near the door. When Brock pulled up, he pushed through the door and ushered her to the vehicle, sweeping his gaze from side to side as she climbed in.

Minutes later, they were on the road, the bright lights from the hospital fading behind them. She took a minute to calm herself, then asked, "Where are we going? Back to the hotel in Timberland Falls?"

The men exchanged a glance. "Yes. But first Steele is going to drop me off," Brock said. "I need to help the team find Neil Otterson."

She told herself it didn't matter if Neil was arrested. Trent couldn't do much until he'd recovered from his injuries. "Wait a minute. What if someone else attacked Trent to put a wrench in his plan to defend Otterson? Like one of Otterson's enemies? The family or friends of the two boys he'd killed?"

Steele turned to flash her a look of admiration. "That's a good theory. I guess we'll know more once Otterson is found and arrested."

She nodded, then turned to look out the window. They were heading toward the precinct, the opposite direction from Timberland Falls. She'd seen more of the city and surrounding suburbs in the past few days than she had in her entire life.

When Brock pulled into the parking lot behind the building, he threw the gearshift into park but kept the engine running. "I'll be in touch," he told Steele.

"Thanks." Steele quickly jumped from the passenger seat to slide behind the wheel. "Harper, sit up front."

"Okay." She did as he'd asked. Less than thirty seconds later, they were back on the road.

"We're taking the long route back to Timberland Falls." Steele glanced at her. "Once we arrive, we're going to stay put until the danger is over."

"And what if that takes weeks?" She shook her head. "Don't make promises you can't keep."

He held her gaze for a moment, and the memory of their heated and all too brief kiss shimmered in the air between them. She had to look away to keep from leaning forward to kiss him again.

"It won't take that long," Steele finally said. "Things are escalating."

She couldn't argue. With Trent injured, she didn't have the same burning need to get back to the office. Not that she couldn't still support Earl Roberts, but he had his own assistant.

Without warning, Steele took a hard right. She let out a squeak, grabbing for the hand rest.

"What's going on?" She was afraid to ask. And even more afraid of the answer.

"We picked up a tail." His gaze darted between the road ahead and the rearview mirror. "Hang on."

Tightening her grip on the hand rest, she planted her feet against the floorboard. Yet she was thrown from side to side when Steele made another series of abrupt turns. Then he sped up, going much faster than the speed limit. He made another jarring turn, then hit the gas to take the nearest on-ramp to the interstate.

"Did we lose him?" She didn't dare turn in her seat to look. Her seat belt had already tightened painfully across her belly. This was hardly the stress-free scenario her doctor had advised.

Lord Jesus, please keep us safe in Your care!

The prayer didn't work, probably because her heart was lodged in her throat as Steele zipped between cars, changing lanes. Then he crossed three lanes of traffic to get back into the right lane.

"I lost him," he said, slowing to a reasonable speed. "It was a black SUV without front license plates."

She willed her pulse to settle. "How were we found?"

"Not sure." He scowled. "I'm nervous about heading back to Timberland Falls."

She shared his concern. He quickly took the next exit, then had to hit the brakes. There was a large semitruck in front of them, moving with what seemed like excruciating slowness.

"Hang on!" The urgency in Steele's voice alarmed her. She risked a glance over her shoulder to see a large SUV coming down the exit ramp toward them.

They were going to die. For some strange reason, she was eerily calm. Almost as if she could hear Jesus calling her home.

Then Steele had his gun out, his window down, and was shooting at the SUV. She gasped as a bullet struck the driver's side of the windshield. The SUV veered off to the side, barely missing their rear bumper. It was going so fast that it flipped over, rolling along the side of the ramp.

Steele ducked back inside the car, put the gearshift in reverse, and backed up. Then he drove up and over the opposite curb to get around the semitruck.

To her horror, another cramp tightened around her abdomen. No, please, no. Not again!

Steele was too preoccupied with getting far away from the crashed SUV to notice. She desperately smoothed her hands over her stomach, struggling to regulate her breathing. Being upset wasn't going to help.

But knowing that didn't stop the tears that filled her eyes. She sniffled and fought them back. But they still rolled down her cheeks.

"Hey, what's wrong?" Steele asked. He was driving insanely fast, taking dozens of turns to put distance between them and the overturned SUV.

"I can't do this anymore . . ." She stifled a sob. "I can't, Steele. I'm going to lose my baby!"

He abruptly turned into a parking lot, driving around to the back side of the building. Then he stopped the car, threw the gearshift into park, and gathered her close. Well, as close as the center console allowed.

"Don't cry. You're safe. Please don't cry." He sounded more upset now than he had when the SUV had been barreling toward them.

She pressed her face into his shoulder, seeking strength. Steele pressed a warm kiss to her temple and continued whispering reassuring words into her ear.

Slowly, she relaxed against him. The cramping in her abdomen eased, which helped. The danger was over. For now.

Ridiculous to wish she could stay cradled in Steele's arms forever.

WATCHING Harper dissolve into tears had hit hard. He felt as if he'd failed her. They'd barely gotten out of the hospital only to land smack in the middle of danger again.

And they were too close to Timberland Falls for comfort. He needed a real safe house for her. This time, he wasn't accepting no as an answer.

After a few minutes Harper sat up, wiping her hands over her face. "I'm a mess."

"You're beautiful." He reached up to tuck a long strand of damp hair behind her ear. "I need to make a few calls, okay?"

She glanced around fearfully. "Are we safe here? What

if the police come looking for us? We caused that car to crash."

He had taken shots at the SUV, not her. But he appreciated her concern. "This will only take a minute." He pulled out his new disposable phone, wondering how the black SUV had found them. Had they been tailed from the hospital? The precinct?

Or all the way from Timberland Falls?

"Steele, will you pray with me?" Harper's tone was tentative.

How could he deny her request? He dropped the phone in the center console and reached for her hand. "Yes, Harper. I'm no expert in the prayer department, though."

"I'm not either." She managed a watery smile. Then she took a deep breath and bowed her head. "Dear Lord, we humbly ask for Your safety and wisdom. Please continue to keep all of us, including all the tactical team members, safe in Your care."

"Amen." A sense of peace washed over him. Something he'd never experienced before after praying.

Not that he'd had much practice. Maybe Rhy and Joe were onto something. Maybe they felt God's presence the way he just had.

"Thanks." She released his hands. "I needed that."

"Me too," he answered honestly.

Her smile brightened, and she sat back in her seat. "Go ahead and make your calls."

He picked up the phone and punched in Rhy's number, assuming his boss was still at the precinct.

"Captain Finnegan," Rhy answered.

"It's Steele. We're in trouble." He quickly explained how the SUV had found and nearly rammed into them. "I shot the windshield on the driver's side. The SUV rolled and stopped. I have no idea if anyone survived."

"I'll get Grayson out there ASAP," Rhy said. "You're both okay?"

"Yeah." He didn't mention Harper's meltdown. "I'm not going back to Timberland Falls. We need that safe house."

"I have Joe in here now too. And Flynn. Hang on, I'll call my brother, Tarin." There was a long pause before he came back on the line. "Okay, you're good to go. Tarin said the place has been vacated. Do you remember the address?"

"Yes." It was a relief to know they could get into the secure home. The bullet-resistant glass would provide a badly needed extra layer of protection.

"Hang on, Joe has more news from the ATF guys." There was another pause, and this time Joe's voice came over the line. "Steele? We have you on speaker."

He glanced at Harper who was listening to his end of the call. He hesitated, then decided she deserved to know what was going on. So much for keeping his professional distance. He placed his phone on speaker and balanced it in the palm of his hand. "Go ahead. What's up?"

"Brady called; they're tracking Otterson's cell phone. He's heading to the Third Ward, not that far from the address Feldman gave us as Tommy Grotto's hideout."

"That's good news." He smiled reassuringly at Harper. "Sounds like you should be able to get a team there to apprehend him."

"That's the plan," Joe agreed. "And the location is interesting, isn't it? We're working with the ATF to uncover a connection between Otterson and Grotto."

Harper frowned and shrugged. She didn't seem to understand how the two crimes could be related either.

"I hope you find something," he said. "I know Milwaukee isn't as big as Chicago, but it does seem strange that both Grotto and Otterson have a connection to the Third Ward."

"Yeah, too much of a coincidence for my peace of mind," Joe agreed. "Are you sure you're not hurt?"

"We're okay." He pursed his lips for a moment. "You know, I'd feel better if Brock or Raelyn or one of the other team members met us at the safe house. It's possible this vehicle is compromised."

"That's not a problem," Joe assured him. "Sounds like Brock is at Gibson and Roberts, working the crime scene, but Raelyn just walked in. Flynn is still on desk duty. I'll have someone meet you there as soon as possible."

"Great, thanks." He felt much better knowing backup was on the way. "Whoever is available is fine with me."

"Oh, one more thing," Rhy spoke up.

"What's that?" He was impatient to hit the road. Tarin's safe house was located near Ravenswood, which was nearly thirty minutes away. And that didn't take into consideration the fact that he'd need to backtrack, making sure they weren't followed.

Again.

"We took another look at the two victims Otterson killed in his so-called carjacking. We'd like you to show the photographs to Harper. See if she recognizes them."

"That's fine with me," Harper spoke for the first time.

"Great. We'll send them in a text to your phone. Let us know if Harper can ID them."

"Got it." He ended the call.

"I doubt I'll recognize them," Harper said with a frown.

"I know." He reached for her hand. "All we ask is that

you do your best. As soon as we review these pictures, we'll head to the safe house."

"I like the sound of that."

He did too. His phone dinged with a text. He opened the message and clicked on the first image. He handed her the phone.

She examined the young man's features closely, then shook her head. "No, sorry."

He didn't show his disappointment. This was a long shot anyway. He took the phone and brought up the next picture.

She frowned, then slowly nodded. "He looks vaguely familiar. He kind of reminds me of one of the photographs you showed me that first day. After I was nearly abducted."

Battling a wave of excitement, he called Rhy back. "Okay, I need Raelyn to send copies of all eighteen photos we showed Harper that first day. Rae put together three six-packs. I need them as soon as possible."

"She'll do that now, before she heads to the safe house."

"Thanks." He lowered the phone, then started the car. It would take her a few minutes to get them together. In the meantime, he could head to Ravenswood.

They drove in silence for several minutes. When his phone began to ping, he waited until it stopped before passing it to Harper. "Take your time. There will be eighteen photos to review."

"Okay." She seemed happy to have something to do. Maybe it would take her mind off her boss's attack and their recent near miss.

He was grateful for his sharpshooting skills, since taking aim at a moving vehicle from an awkward position wasn't easy. He made a mental note to head back to the range once this was over. Maybe Jina was onto something with her constant practicing.

He drove onto the interstate, heading in the opposite direction for several miles before getting off and getting back on again. He didn't see anyone following them but kept his gaze sharp as he headed toward Ravenswood.

Harper was still reviewing mug shots. Eighteen pictures on a small phone screen were a lot to get through. Yet he noticed she was quick to finish with some but then spent a much longer period of time with others.

Anticipation rippled through him. Maybe they should have considered a link between Otterson and her ex-husband's gunrunning business sooner.

"Okay, you might think I'm crazy, but there's a photograph here that I thought looked somewhat familiar before." She turned the screen toward him. He was shocked to see Tommy Grotto's face. "But he's not Hispanic, like the two guys who were killed."

He was confused. "Okay, then how is he familiar?"

"He has some facial features that remind me of Neil Otterson." She flushed and shrugged. "I didn't make that connection back when the abduction happened. But the more I look at him now, the more I see a resemblance to Neil Otterson."

"You mean, he could be a relative? A nephew, half brother, or son?" he asked.

"I know it sounds crazy. But they have the same eyes, the same cleft chin. I don't know, maybe it's just my imagination."

"Show me the picture again." He wished they had a photo of Neil Otterson to compare it to. He'd looked at the guy's mug shot, but that was a while ago.

She turned the phone toward him.

"Okay, you could be right. But what about the Hispanic victim? I thought you said he looked familiar?"

"I know, hang on." She went back to looking through the phone. "The first victim looks a little like this picture too."

That mug shot she showed him wasn't familiar, as far as being involved in the case. But that doesn't mean the two men weren't connected in some way. Maybe they were brothers or cousins who were both involved in the drug running operation. And maybe it wasn't Tommy Grotto who was in charge but Neil Otterson.

"Okay, do me a favor and text Rhy back with your observations. They can dig a little deeper into extended family connections between both pairs of men."

"Okay." She tapped the keys on his phone. He exited the interstate, choosing to take several side streets before reaching the safe house.

Less than thirty seconds passed before his phone rang. He gestured for Harper to answer.

"This is Harper answering Steele's phone. Hang on, I'll put you on speaker."

"It's Rhy. We're digging into the possible connection between Otterson and Tommy Grotto and the two Hispanic men. I put a call in to the two ATF agents watching over Feldman too."

"You think Feldman knows Neil Otterson?" He wished he'd asked the perp when they'd had the opportunity.

"It's worth a shot. But the better news is that Neil Otterson has been taken into custody. He's not talking," Rhy said quickly. "But we have him off the street."

"That's the best news of the day," Steele agreed.

"I'm hoping we can get Otterson to open up now that he has more charges pending against him," Rhy said, his tone ringing with satisfaction. "And once Trent Gibson wakes up, he should be able to let us know if Otterson was the one who assaulted him."

"He's doing okay?" Harper asked.

"He's being evaluated in the emergency department but has regained consciousness," Rhy answered.

"Praise the Lord," Harper whispered.

"Yes," Rhy agreed.

Steele spoke up. "We're heading to the safe house. Did Raelyn leave yet?"

"About five minutes ago." The sound of a phone ringing could be heard in the background. "I have to go. Michaels is on the other line."

"Later, then." He glanced at Harper who pushed the end call button. "You did good work, Harper."

"I hope so." She shook her head. "I honestly never believed Neil Otterson was involved."

"We didn't either." They drove in silence for a long fifteen minutes. The traffic wasn't too bad, which helped. When he reached the safe house, he drove past without stopping. There were no cars parked anywhere nearby, and the place appeared empty. After circling the block, he pulled into the driveway and shut down the engine. "Let's get you inside."

"How do we access the place?" She pushed open her door.

"There's a push button lock on the front door." He quickly escorted her up the sidewalk. It had been recently shoveled, which was nice. He entered the four-digit number provided by Joe, then pushed the door open.

The inside was nice, nothing fancy, but clean and serviceable. He shut the door behind him, then removed his jacket from Harper, tossing it aside.

"This is nice," she said, gazing around. "I was expecting something smaller and more dungeonlike."

The sound of a footstep on the floor made him turn toward the hallway. He froze when Steve Banner emerged, holding a gun leveled at his chest. "Don't move. One step and I'll shoot. At this point, I have nothing to lose."

Steele didn't move a muscle, but his mind raced. Steve Banner had never been a suspect. But it was clear he'd been wrong about the ATF agent all along.

And he feared Harper would pay the ultimate price for his mistake.

CHAPTER FIFTEEN

This was it. They were going to die here today. Harper was stunned to see Steve Banner holding a gun on them. If either of the ATF agents were involved, she'd have felt certain the culprit would have been Bryon Perkins. Although for all she knew, he was here too.

"Toss down your weapon," Banner ordered. "Slowly. One false move and I'll shoot the baby."

Banner shifted, moving the barrel of the gun toward her abdomen. Her breath caught in her throat, and it was all she could do not to curl into a ball and scream.

"Okay. I hear you. No one needs to get shot today." Steele slowly pulled his gun from his holster and bent to drop it on the floor.

"Kick it to me." Banner continued to point his gun at her belly.

Steele kicked it with enough force that the gun slid past him. Banner narrowed his gaze but let it go.

"Now your backup weapon." Banner sneered. "Ankle holster, right?"

"I don't have a backup on me." Steele pulled the fabric of his uniform pants to show his ankles.

Banner frowned as if trying to decide whether this was a trick. Then he shrugged. "Fine, then toss your utility belt down too. And the knife I'm sure you have in your pocket."

Steele complied.

"What do you want?" Harper found her voice. She knew Steele had arranged for Raelyn to meet them here. She hoped that keeping Banner talking would give the female officer time to get here.

And then? She had no idea how they'd get out of this alive.

"I want the evidence you have about the drug running scheme, specifically my complicity within the operation." Banner's gaze bored into hers. "And I want it now."

Seriously? The man was delusional. "I don't have anything. You know that. You and Perkins searched my apartment."

"You have it hidden somewhere else," Banner said. His gaze dropped to her belly, then back up. "You're going to tell me where it is. Or I'll kill that kid."

Honestly, she would gladly hand over whatever he wanted if she had a clue what he was talking about. "I don't have it. Why would you even think I did?"

"Because Ellis Starkey said he hid something where only you would know where to find it." Banner took a threatening step toward her. "Enough playing games. I'm only going to ask you one more time. Where is it?"

"She doesn't know anything," Steele said.

"Starkey claimed she does." An evil smile tipped up the corner of Banner's mouth. "Right before I shot him."

Steve Banner had murdered Ellis. Not Tommy Grotto or anyone else within the gunrunning organization. An

ATF agent sworn to uphold the law had cold-bloodedly ended Ellis's life.

And she had no doubt he would kill them too.

The image of the blue vase Ellis had given her flashed in her mind. If he had hidden anything inside, it was likely ruined by the water she'd used for her wildflowers. Unless there was something hidden in the base?

It was the only possibility that made any sense. "Okay, okay." She splayed her palms over her belly, as if that alone would protect her baby. Ignoring Steele's shocked gaze, she said, "it's in the blue vase in my apartment."

Banner scowled. "We checked the vase. It was empty except for the plastic flowers."

"You didn't check the base." She forced herself to hold his gaze. "Ellis Starkey gave me that vase. He hid something in the base."

"Well, well." Banner made a *tsk-tsk* sound. "I guess he was smarter than I gave him credit for."

"Go to my apartment. Get the vase and check the bottom." She fought to keep her voice steady. "You'll find whatever you're looking for."

"You don't need us," Steele added.

"Nice try. But it's too late. You both have to die." Banner's tone was matter of fact. "Don't worry, I'll make sure to frame Tommy Grotto for this too."

"Where is Grotto?" Steele asked. She sensed he was stalling, waiting for Raelyn to arrive.

"He's alive if that's what you're getting at." Banner shrugged. "Not Waylon, though. After he failed to grab you off the street, he took a long walk off a short pier." Banner let out a harsh laugh at his own pathetic joke. "Tommy still has his uses, or he'd be dead at the bottom of Lake Michigan as well. Too bad his old man managed to get himself arrested again. I told Tommy to kill him and be done with it, but he couldn't bring himself to do it."

Just as she'd thought, the similarity between Neil Otterson and Tommy Grotto was because they shared DNA. Father and son. And Banner was so heartless he'd wanted Tommy to kill his own father.

Banner was a monster. One who looked and behaved normally but had a black heart.

She silently prayed that Raelyn would get there soon.

Steele twisted a bit and abruptly stepped into the gap between her and the ATF agent.

Banner laughed. "This gun is loaded with tungsten carbide bullets. You have no chance of surviving this, despite wearing your vest. And once you're out of the way, I'll get rid of the preggo."

A glimpse of a small gun in Steele's hand caught her eye. Where had he gotten it? Somewhere within his vest? Regardless, she knew what he was going to do. She instantly dropped to the floor, curling into a ball just as twin gunshots echoed around her.

From the corner of her eye, she saw the front door burst open revealing Brock and Raelyn. The two tactical team officers ran inside and took control of the situation. They surrounded a bleeding Banner, removing the gun from his hand and placing him under arrest. Then they moved through the rest of the house, making sure no one else was there.

As they did that, she lifted her head, searching for Steele. He was standing just a few feet away, but there was also a small pool of bright red blood on the floor.

He was hit? She forced herself to stand on her shaky legs. "You're bleeding!"

"Yeah, he caught me in the calf." Steele turned toward

her. "I'm sorry. I don't know how this happened. Banner and Perkins shouldn't have known anything about this safe house."

"It's not your fault." She took a step toward him. As if understanding her need, he drew her close, giving her a hug. "I was so scared. Where did you get that second gun?"

"I had it tucked beneath the vest, it's a trick we sometimes do. Easier to grab it from there rather than the ankle holster." He buried his face against her hair for a long moment. "There was no way I was going to let him hurt you or the baby."

Overwhelming relief washed over her. She leaned against him for a moment, then forced herself to step back. "I need to tend to your wound."

"It's fine." He waved a dismissive hand.

"There's an ambulance on the way," Raelyn spoke up as she and Brock returned. "Banner needs it more than you. Do you want me to call for a second rig?"

"No." He shook his head. "I'll slap a bandage on it later."

"Better do it now. You're trailing blood all over the place," Brock drawled.

With a grimace, Steele limped past the prone figure of Banner toward the hallway where she assumed the bathroom was located.

Banner's gaze locked on hers. The malevolence reflected there gave her pause. She turned toward Brock. "What about his partner?"

"Strangely, Perkins is back at the precinct questioning Otterson." Brock shrugged. "He claimed he was waiting for Banner to show up. It could be Banner is in this alone, but trust me, we'll dig deeper to see if Perkins is involved."

It was another hard lesson not to trust a person by their

outward appearance. Or the way they portrayed themselves to others. She should have known that already from Jake, but apparently, she was a slow learner. Banner had come across as supportive but would not have hesitated to kill her.

Banner remained silent, but she could see the wheels spinning in his mind. No doubt, he'd try to come up with a plan to implicate Perkins or to exonerate himself.

She hoped the danger was finally over. Banner must have orchestrated the attacks against her with Grotto's help. All because of the evidence Ellis may have hidden in the blue vase.

"We need to get to my apartment as soon as possible." She was proud of her calm tone. "Banner made it clear he was looking for evidence that Starkey hid from him. I think it may be hidden in the bottom of the blue vase."

Brock looked surprised, then nodded. "Yeah, okay." He glanced over as Steele returned from tending his wound.

"I agree with Harper. We need that vase."

"Call Rhy, have him send someone," Raelyn suggested. "Until we know Perkins isn't involved or that Grotto isn't lurking nearby, you should stay here."

"Yeah, okay." Steele's expression was glum. "I guess I messed up enough for one day."

"I think Flynn may have been the one to mess up," Brock said. "He was in Rhy's office today when you called to get the safe house. Including the code Tarin had provided for you to get inside."

"And Flynn may have mentioned it to Banner because the guy saved his life." Steele groaned. "He's going to kick himself when he learns the truth."

"Yeah. He will." Brock managed a smile. "Or maybe he'll let you kick him."

Steele rolled his eyes. He pulled out his phone and

made the call to Rhy about the blue vase, giving him every-thing they'd learned from Banner about Tommy Grotto and Otterson being father and son.

Since it appeared they weren't going anywhere soon, she dropped into the closest chair.

She did her best not to break down crying over the fact that her time with Steele was over.

———

STEELE WAS IRRITATED at how he'd allowed Banner to get the drop on them. He'd never expected the bad guys to be waiting inside the safe house.

And he should have. At the very least, he should have waited outside for Raelyn to arrive.

His calf wound throbbed, but he was thankful it was a minor injury. If Banner wasn't lying about the tungsten carbide slugs, this showdown could have ended badly.

The ambulance arrived. There was a flurry of activity as the paramedics rushed in to provide care for Steve Banner. He recognized the friendly face of Colin Finnegan, but other than giving him a nod in return, the firefighter slash paramedic quickly turned his attention to the wounded man.

Steele limped over to where Harper sat at the kitchen table. Now that the immediate threat had been neutralized, she looked shell-shocked. Her palms were spread protec-tively over her belly.

"Have the cramps returned?" He dropped to one knee beside her. "We can call that second ambulance if you need to go back to the hospital."

"No need, I'm fine." Then she shook her head. "That's a

lie. I'm not fine. I can't believe Banner is one of the bad guys. And that he shot you."

"The worst part was when he threatened you," he said softly. "And your baby."

She nodded. "Selfishly, I was worried about my baby. I guess the good news is that I don't have any cramping."

"I'm so sorry," he murmured. "I never wanted you to be in harm's way."

"It's not your fault." She drew in a long, deep breath. "But I'll be glad when the danger is over for good."

"Rhy is taking Perkins into custody until he's cleared. And Rhy let me know that Otterson was spilling details on Tommy Grotto too. He even admitted to striking out at Gibson, hitting him in the head when he discovered there was an arrest warrant issued for him." He shook his head. "Sounds like Grotto had more loyalty for his old man than the other way around."

"It's horrible to think that a father would turn against his son," she said.

"Don't worry, we'll find Grotto. Rhy has the entire team scattered in different directions to help tie up the loose ends."

She lifted her gaze to his. "Once Tommy Grotto is arrested, the danger will be over for good."

"Yeah." He wrapped his arms around her slim shoulders and hugged her. Harper deserved to get back to her old life. Steele wanted nothing more than for her to be safe, to have her baby in peace.

Yet he also didn't want to let her go.

He'd fallen in love with her. That moment he'd stepped in front of her to face off with Banner, he'd fully expected to die. He hadn't cared about that as long as he could take Banner down with him.

Long enough for Harper to escape.

"Let's get him out of here." Colin's voice reached his ears. He turned in time to see Colin and another paramedic wheel Steve Banner out of the safe house. There was no denying the spurt of satisfaction in seeing Banner's ankle cuffed to the gurney.

"I'm coming with you," Brock said.

"No argument here," Colin agreed.

Raelyn followed them outside, leaving them alone. Maybe she'd sensed that he needed some time with Harper.

"I love you." He hadn't meant to blurt the words out like that, but he couldn't regret them either.

"You—what?" Her green eyes widened. "That's not possible."

"It is possible. I love you." The words came easier this time. "I understand you may not feel the same way. But at the very least, I would ask that you come and stay with me for a few weeks. In the guest room," he hastily added. "And just long enough to be sure that all of the people involved in the gunrunning organization have been arrested."

A flare of exasperation darkened her eyes. "I don't want or need your pity or charity. I'm perfectly capable of getting a second part-time job as a server if needed."

"I don't pity you, and this isn't about charity." He tried to soften his sharp tone. "I love you, Harper. You're a strong woman who showed me what it is like to have faith in God."

She shook her head. "You don't know what you're saying. I'm pregnant. No sane man would want to be with a woman about to give birth to another man's child."

"The baby is yours, and I will love him or her no matter what."

She continued shaking her head. "That doesn't make sense. I trust you, but I don't have anything to offer you."

Okay, now she was making him mad. "You have yourself, Harper. Your beauty, inside and out. Your sweet kindness. And don't sit there and pretend you don't feel anything for me." He lifted her chin, forcing her to meet his gaze. "I've kissed you. Twice."

Her gaze landed on his mouth. He smiled and leaned forward, capturing her lips with his. She melted against him, and he gathered her as close as he could in their awkward position.

"Ahem." Someone cleared their throat loudly from the doorway. Inwardly railing at the rotten timing, he lifted his head to scowl at Rhy.

"Go away."

"We have the vase." Rhy, of course, ignored him. Joe stepped over the threshold behind him, carrying the large blue vase. "We thought you'd want to be a part of finding out what's inside."

He did, but they could have given him another five minutes. Or ten. Or twenty.

With a sigh, he rose to his feet. "Of course, I want to find out what is inside."

"Me too," Harper chimed in.

"To be fair, we haven't found anything yet," Joe said, setting it on the table. "Our arms aren't skinny enough to reach the bottom. Rather than smash it into pieces we thought you might want to try, Harper."

She rose and stuck her hand into the vase. "The bottom feels smooth. I'm worried that whatever is down there has been ruined by water."

"Check along the edges," Steele said. "It's a vase. Starkey may have wrapped something in plastic beneath it."

"Hang on." She twisted her arm one way, then another.

"I think I have it." She slowly pulled her hand from the vase, holding what appeared to be a false bottom.

"Is there something else in there?" Rhy asked.

"Yes, but I needed to get this out of the way." Harper slid her arm back into the vase and brought out a small plastic bag. "Look! There's a small USB drive inside."

"Joe, grab the computer from the SUV." Rhy grinned. "Good work, Harper."

Steele wrapped his arm around Harper's waist. Rhy arched a brow but didn't say anything. When Joe returned with the computer, they inserted the drive and opened the file.

"Jackpot," Rhy said with satisfaction. "Dates, names, amounts of money that exchanged hands. And we even have information here on the contacts in Detroit and Chicago."

"By the way, Banner admitted to killing Waylon Brooks," he said.

"That would explain why we haven't found him yet. And that's why the FBI is taking over the investigation," Rhy said. "The ATF is tainted by Banner's involvement. I'm sure the FBI offices in both Detroit and Chicago will dig into the gunrunning on their turf."

Steele nodded. It was the absolute best outcome they could have asked for. Short of getting everyone arrested in one fell swoop. He tapped the screen. "I don't see Perkins listed in here."

"No, but I won't release him from custody until we dig further." A shadow crossed Rhy's features. "I feel terrible about all this. Flynn shouldn't have revealed the location of the safe house, much less the code to get in. He feels awful about the role he inadvertently played. He offered to resign from the team."

"It's not his fault." Steele frowned. "Don't let him resign. He's a good cop. I'm sure his view of Banner was tainted because the guy saved his life."

"Flynn owns that too. And it's a tough lesson for all of us. I hope to convince Flynn to stay." Rhy gestured to the laptop. "We have enough evidence here that I'm not so sure we need Feldman's testimony."

"The feds made a deal, though," Steele pointed out. "I doubt they can back out of it."

"That depends. We now know Banner is dirty. Maybe his involvement in all of this will negate part of the deal. And there's always the possibility Feldman was holding back on us. That could make the deal null and void too." Rhy removed the USB drive and closed the laptop. "Either way, we'll make sure Feldman doesn't cause any trouble for Harper."

"Thank you." Harper smiled. "I appreciate that."

Rhy and Joe turned away. Harper was about to follow, but he caught her hand in his. "Harper? Will you at least consider coming to my place for a few days?"

She turned to face him. "Are you sure about this?"

"Yes." He hesitated, then drew her into his arms. "Give me a chance to prove how much I love you."

"Oh, Steele." She shook her head, but a smile kicked up the corner of her mouth. "I've made bad decisions in the past. I'm worried that you'll regret this, and I'll end up hurt."

"I won't regret this or hurt you." He hesitated, then said, "After Monique's death, I didn't think I would ever love a woman again. But I was wrong. I love you. Just give me time to prove how much."

She searched his gaze for a long moment, then sighed. "What am I going to do with you?"

"Kiss me again?" he asked hopefully.

She wound her arms around his neck. "I love kissing you."

He figured that was a start. He kissed her again until they were both breathless. Then he rested his forehead on hers. "I want to share my life with you."

"And a screaming, crying baby?" Doubt laced her tone.

"Yes." He lifted his head to look down at her. "I want you, Harper. All I'm asking for is a chance."

She searched his gaze again for a long moment. "I didn't want to fall in love with you, Steele. But I did."

"Hallelujah," he whispered. "You've made me a happy man, Harper."

"Hold on a minute." She frowned. "I'm not sure you've thought this through. That you understand what a future with me entails."

"I know my heart, Harper. With love, we can conquer anything."

She considered him for a long moment. "I'm thankful God sent you to rescue me that first day."

"Me too," he admitted. "And I promise I won't rush you into anything. We have plenty of time. I want you to be sure about this too."

"I honestly can't imagine a future without you," she admitted. "And that feels selfish. As if I need you more than you need me."

"Yeah, that's not possible." He pulled her close. "You're everything I've ever wanted. I just didn't know it until God threw us together."

She chuckled. "That He did."

"Let's get out of here." He smiled, thrilled that she was giving him a chance. "Will you please come to my house until we know it's safe?"

"Yes, I'll come with you." She paused, then added, "For now."

"For now and forever, if I have anything to say about it." He gave her another quick kiss, then stepped back. Maintaining control around her would prove to be difficult. But he was up for the challenge. "Let's go."

"Now and forever, huh?" She laughed and took his hand. "Let's just take things one day at a time."

One day at a time for the rest of their lives was fine with him. Because now that he had Harper in his arms, he never wanted to let her go.

EPILOGUE

Two months later . . .

"Come on, push." As much as she adored the sweet Dr. Webb, this drill sergeant of a labor and delivery nurse was dancing on her last nerve.

"I'm trying." She panted and pushed as hard as she could with Steele's arm supporting her from behind.

"You're strong. God is with you. You can do this." His whispered words of encouragement were amazing, but she wasn't in the mood.

She wanted this baby to be born. Now!

"One more," the nurse encouraged. "Push with the next contraction."

Easy for the nurse to say. She wasn't sweating and writhing in pain. Harper tried not to snap.

Dr. Webb stepped into the room, offering a reassuring smile. "Everything looks good."

Grinding her teeth together, she waited for the next contraction. Pain nearly overwhelmed her, but she gathered every bit of strength she had left and pushed.

"There's the head." Dr. Webb's eyes crinkled with a

smile behind his face mask. "One more contraction should do it."

One more? She panted, gazing up at Steele. He kissed her forehead. "You're strong, Harper. You can do this."

She didn't feel strong. She wanted to scream at all these people to leave her alone. But of course, that wasn't an option. There was no reverse button on this having a baby gig. The next contraction began to build, and there was no time to do anything but push.

"There she is, a beautiful baby girl." Dr. Webb beamed as if he'd done the work. The baby cried, and this time she let the tears come.

A baby girl!

"Amelia," she whispered.

Steele looked at her in surprise. "Really? You want to name her after my sister?"

"Yes, Amelia Rose." She watched as the drill sergeant nurse cleaned the baby, then brought her daughter over for skin-to-skin contact. She tucked the baby into the V neck of her gown and pressed a kiss to the baby's head. Steele placed his warm palm over the baby's back as if the three of them were a real family.

And maybe they were. Fighting her love for him was useless. Not that they hadn't had the occasional argument, because they had. Mostly over her wanting to do things and Steele insisting she rest.

He could be bossy and overprotective. He liked things done his way. Yet he was also loving and caring and gentle in a way she'd never experienced before.

She'd resigned from the Gibson and Roberts law firm after confronting Trent about the billing inconsistencies. She had thankfully gotten another position as an administrative assistant in the administrative building downtown.

She liked working for the ADAs, especially Maddy Sinclair and Bax Scala.

She glanced up in alarm as another contraction hit. How could she have forgotten the afterbirth?

"Hold her, will you?" She lifted Amelia Rose toward Steele. He quickly unbuttoned his shirt and held the baby against his bare chest.

Watching him gaze at Amelia in awe made her realize she was being foolish to wait. Just because she'd made a mistake with Jake didn't mean she wasn't choosing wisely this time.

After delivering the placenta, she rested back against the pillow.

Steele leaned forward, handing the baby back to her. "You've made me so happy, Harper. Will you please marry me?"

This was the third time he'd asked her. The first was after Tommy Grotto had been arrested. Then again when they'd learned the feds discovered Jake had held back key information specifically about Banner's involvement in the scheme, negating his original deal for witness protection. They'd transferred Jake to a different prison for his safety, but he'd serve his time.

As he should.

And again now. Maybe the third time was the charm. She didn't see any reason to hold off. She loved him. And finally accepted he must love her too. Why? She wasn't sure. She smiled and nodded. "Yes, Steele. I would be thrilled to marry you."

"Thank You, God." He captured her mouth in a quick kiss, then let out a whoop. "I'm going to be a great husband and father."

"I know you will." She had no doubt about that. "And I promise to be a great wife and mother."

He leaned forward, placed his hand on Amelia's back, and kissed her temple. "Our family."

She couldn't imagine a better way to bring a new baby into the world.

I HOPE you enjoyed Steele and Harper's story in *Steele*. I'm really excited about this new series. Are you ready to read about Brock and Liana in *Brock*? Click here!

DEAR READER

Thanks so much for reading *Steele*, the first book in my new Oath of Honor series. I'm having so much fun weaving the Finnegans into these stories. It's a great way to stay caught up with what's going on in their lives.

If you liked this book, I hope you give *Brock* a try. I plan to write a book for each of the members of the tactical team. You won't want to miss any of these exciting stories.

Don't forget, you can purchase eBooks or audiobooks directly from my website, and you will receive a 15% discount by using the code **LauraScott15**.

I adore hearing from my readers! I can be found through my website at https://www.laurascottbooks.com, via Facebook at https://www.facebook.com/LauraScott Books, Instagram at https://www.instagram.com/laurascott books/, and Twitter https://twitter.com/laurascottbooks. Please take a moment to subscribe to my YouTube channel at youtube.com/@LauraScottBooks-wr1xl?sub_confirmation=1. Also, take a moment to sign up for my monthly newsletter to learn about my new book releases! All subscribers receive a free novella not available for purchase on any platform.

Until next time,

Laura Scott

PS Read on for a sneak peek of *Brock*.

BROCK

Chapter One

Police officer Brock Greer stood on the rocky shoreline overlooking Lake Michigan, ignoring the cold March wind blasting his face while trying to shake off his despair. He shouldn't have canceled the appointment with his lawyer. He should just file the divorce paperwork and be done with it.

It was some sort of weakness inside of him that prevented him from taking that final step to end a marriage that had barely begun. He hadn't seen Liana since she'd left him four months ago, after their huge fight when he'd caught a glimpse of her text message with a guy named Troy agreeing to meet up the following day.

He'd accused her of cheating. She'd asked why he didn't trust her, then had turned and walked out of their condo. The morning after their heated exchange, she'd simply texted a brief message. *This won't work. I'm sorry.*

And that was that.

For long minutes, he was numb to the icy blast washing

over him. It matched the coldness in his heart. But he finally turned, hunched his shoulders, and walked toward the city. It wasn't smart to come back to the places he and Liana had been together. Living in their Third Ward condo was hard enough.

The condo was too far away to walk from here. He'd have to grab a rideshare. His stomach rumbled with hunger, he'd skipped lunch again, so he forced himself head to the closest restaurant to grab something to eat.

His feet took him strait to Lu Chen's, a Chinese restaurant that had been one of Liana's favorites. He almost turned away to find someplace else, but then stubbornly opened the door and stepped inside.

He liked Lu Chen's food; they had a wide selection of authentic meals to choose from. He stood in the doorway, looking around the place to make sure Liana wasn't there. He didn't really expect to find her seated in the small dining room. He'd come here often those first few weeks after she'd left him but hadn't found her.

Tonight was no different. Although he was keenly aware of several customers openly staring at him. It took a moment to realize he was still wearing his uniform. The suspicion in their dark gazes made him sigh.

Whatever. He wouldn't be there long enough for his career to be a problem. He ordered his favorite meal as a takeout, then wove his way through the restaurant toward the restrooms. He stopped abruptly when he heard low voices speaking in rapid-fire Chinese.

Too fast for him to understand; besides, he was rusty from lack of practice over these past few months. Liana had taught him the basics, but what he heard now sounded like total gibberish.

He couldn't explain why he'd pushed open the

swinging door to the kitchen. Maybe it was the female voice that lured him in. He frowned and stepped in farther.

"Get out!" The words in furious English were aimed at him. His eyes widened when he saw a tall Asian man and a beautiful mixed-race Asian woman. She looked just like Liana.

She was Liana!

"No police!" The tall Asian abruptly grabbed Liana and pressed a gun to her temple. Brock's jaw dropped as Liana stared at him with annoyance. "Get out! Now!"

"Okay, remain calm, there's no reason to panic." He lifted his hands palms forward to show he wasn't a threat, even as icy fingers of fear ran down his back. What was going on? Why was Liana here? And why was this man threatening to kill her?

"I'm warning you." The Asian man's gaze bored into his as he spoke in a low, threatening tone. "You will turn and leave now. Or she is dead."

"I'm leaving." His hostage negotiation skills were failing him, big time. Brock prided himself on talking people down from the ledge, but this guy was intently focused on the mission at hand. And he had the distinct feeling the Asian would kill Liana without a second thought. He took a half-step backward, forcing a calm serenity into his voice that he was far from feeling. "There's no reason to hurt her. This is all a big misunderstanding. I only came for dinner, nothing more."

The Asian scowled and pressed the gun more firmly against Liana's temple, using enough force to make her wince. Brock took another step back. They were too far away for him to do anything but retreat. He noticed the kitchen staff darted a few quick glances in his direction, but then returned to their work of chopping and cooking.

As if there wasn't anything unusual about seeing a man holding a gun at a woman's head, threatening to shoot.

"I don't know what's going on here. I took a wrong turn, I only wanted to use the restrooms. I don't want any trouble." One more step backward and he'd be out of the kitchen space, and the door would swing shut. Brock hesitated, unwilling to simply leave Liana in this man's hands. Yet what choice did he have?

Liana spoke in Chinese, and this time he caught part of what she was saying. *You're being stupid, he's not here because of us.*

Us? As in the tall Asian was Troy? The man she'd left him for?

Brock turned away, to his right, so that he could subtly reach for his weapon. A blur of movement caught the corner of his eye. Yanking his gun free of the holster, he dropped to one knee and brought the weapon around. Liana must have caught the Asian off guard because she'd twisted out of his grasp and held the gun she'd taken from him.

"Go!" She almost spat the word at Brock. "Leave us!"

Leave them? Not happening. Brock didn't understand what was going on here, but he wasn't leaving her with a man who'd threatened to kill her. Instead, he rushed forward, taking the guy's other arm and wrenching it behind his back.

Drawing handcuffs from his utility belt, he proceeded to slap the silver bracelets on the Asian man's wrists. Liana heaved a sigh and stepped back and tossed the Asian man's weapon onto the closest surface.

"Why are you here?" Her voice was a low hiss as she raked her free hand through her long, straight black hair. "Do you realize what you've done?"

"I came to get dinner." He finished cuffing the man,

then turned to look at her. "And yeah, looks like I may have saved your life."

"Not even close!" She took a step toward him, her dark eyes flashing with anger. "You blew my cover."

Her cover? He shook his head as if unable to comprehend what she was saying. "What cover? What are you talking about?"

She sighed and tipped her head back to stare at the ceiling as if seeking wisdom in the face of his stupidity. And in that moment, he understood.

Liana had been working as an undercover police officer.

DESPITE HER ANNOYANCE at how Brock had burst into the kitchen, sending Bai Chow into panic mode and ultimately blowing her cover, Liana had to admit it was good to see him. She'd missed Brock terribly.

More than she'd thought possible. But not enough to distract her from the mission.

The way he stared at her in complete shock made her realize he hadn't known anything about the op. And if that was true, why was he here?

"You're working undercover?" Brock's tone was incredulous. "All this time? Ever since you left?"

"Yes." She swallowed a sigh, knowing her handler would not be happy about this latest turn of event. Months of work was about to be flushed down the drain.

"Get him out of here." She waved at Bai. "Book him for menacing with a deadly weapon. I have to go."

"Where?" Brock shoved Bai aside and took a step toward her. "Don't you think you owe me an explanation?"

"Not really." She did, of course, but not here. And not now. "Later, okay? We'll meet at PK's."

He shook his head, taking another step forward. "Nope. Don't trust you'll show. In fact, I'd bet my pension that you won't come."

His comment hurt, although she understood why he was leery. Leaving him hadn't been easy. But it had been a necessity. She held his gaze, willing him to believe her. "I promise I'll be at PK's in one hour."

Brock reached for her arm, but she moved quickly, avoiding his grasp. Then she turned and fled through the kitchen, heading for the back door. She felt certain he wouldn't follow, not when he had Bai Chow in custody.

Outside, the cold air made her shiver. Her mind whirled as she tried to come up with a mitigation strategy. The kitchen staff at Lu Chen's were well trained to ignore anything that happened on the premises. As far as she could tell, they hadn't paid her and Bai's altercation any attention. Not even when he'd pulled a gun on her. Yet the Chinese people in general were extremely wary of the police. It would not go over well that a cop had entered the kitchen, taking their restaurant manager into custody.

Think. She needed to think! She couldn't lose the ground she'd gained over the past few months.

Bringing her one step closer to the man only known as Twisted Snake, the leader of the sex-trafficking operation.

And to saving Mai Shi's life.

Darting through streets and back alleys, Liana tried to come up with a plausible excuse. One that would protect her cover. She could try to turn the tables on Bai. To make it sound as if he'd led the police to the restaurant. She had been there first, with Bai arriving fifteen minutes later.

She nodded to herself as she walked swiftly through the

street. Yes, she may be able to make the scenario work.

Unless Bai Chow decided to talk. She inwardly winced. If that happened? There would be no way to salvage the operation.

When she'd put at least a mile between herself and the restaurant, she pulled out her disposable phone. She slowed her pace and did her best to calm her breathing. After a long moment, she made the call.

"Bai was followed to Lu," she said, using the abbreviated version of the restaurant's name. "The police arrived."

The curse on the other end of the phone was slightly reassuring. So far, so good.

"Of course, he was frisked, and his weapon confiscated. He was arrested on the spot," she continued. "I managed to slip out the back."

"Stay out of sight," the male voice instructed her. "I will be in touch."

"Soon, I hope," she agreed. Then she quickly disconnected from the call. If she pressed too much, it would look suspicious.

Even now, she couldn't be sure Muchin had believed her version of events. She swallowed hard and shook her head. What had possessed Brock to show up at the restaurant? To come into the kitchen of all things?

She abruptly stopped. Had he been following her?

No, she always made sure there was no one behind her. And she felt certain Brock's surprise in seeing her had been real.

Rotten timing, she thought with a sigh. Or maybe divine intervention.

Working undercover meant she couldn't attend church services. Or follow any of her old routines in her previous life. Most of the time she didn't even think about her real identity. She'd become Feng Chi in her mind. Not Liana Wong.

But seeing Brock had brought memories of their time together cascading over her like warm waves washing over the shore, reminding her of the wonderful life she'd turned her back on.

The love they'd shared. Well, at least on her part.

She turned a corner and nearly ran into a large African American man. Murmuring an apology in Chinese, she attempted to skirt around him.

A beefy hand shot out and grabbed her arm. She whirled and lashed out with her foot, kicking him in the groin. He instantly released her, letting out a howl of pain.

As he doubled over, cursing at her, Liana broke into a run, putting badly needed distance between them. She was annoyed with herself for letting her guard down. This area of the city that had become her home turf wasn't exactly a nice part of town.

She needed to keep her wits about her. No more thinking about Brock until she made it to PK's.

Liana turned down her street, keeping a sharp eye out for anyone lingering nearby. She needed to get her vehicle, a rusty sedan that looked to be on its last leg but had a decent engine, thanks to the undercover squad at MPD. And she also needed to grab her weapon. Normally, she didn't carry one, as that wasn't part of her role. Yet she couldn't be sure Muchin would believe her story. If he didn't and decided to send someone after her, she needed to be ready.

She really, really wished Brock hadn't blown her cover.

Slipping into her apartment building, she took the stairs to the second floor. She paused outside her door, listening intently before putting her key in the lock and pushing the door open.

Standing off to the side, she peered quickly around the doorjamb to scan the room. Nothing seemed out of place. She always took care to scatter items around in what appeared to be haphazard way.

But she knew exactly where every item was supposed to be.

Reassured her apartment hadn't been breached and searched, she ducked inside and closed the door behind her. Then she cautiously crept toward the hallway where the bedroom and bathroom were located.

Both were empty.

There was no time to waste. She entered her bedroom and quickly used a screwdriver to open a panel in her window air conditioner to retrieve her service weapon. Not the most original hiding spot in the world, but the stark apartment didn't offer many options.

Then she grabbed her keys from beneath a pile of mail and headed back outside. This part of the city didn't have luxuries like underground parking. Or any parking lots. There was only street parking that was on a first-come-first-serve basis. And in winter, the rule of parking on only one side of the street, alternating days to make room for snow-plows, made those precious parking spaces even more difficult to find.

Her vehicle was four blocks away, but she didn't head straight there. Taking her usual surveillance precautions, she headed in the opposite direction for three blocks before circling back, her sharp gaze making sure she hadn't been followed.

By the time she reached her sedan, her fingers were numb from the cold. She only wore thin gloves and a worn coat, in keeping with her disguise of living in a low-income neighborhood and had to blow into her cupped palms to warm up before she could get inside the vehicle.

All this because Brock had stumbled into her meeting with Bai.

Rather than scraping the ice from her windshield, she sat in the car and waited for it to melt. Then she had to finagle the car back and forth to get out of the tight space, before heading to the Third Ward.

Patty's Kitchen was a small diner not far from the condo she once shared with Brock. They had shared many pancake breakfasts there and the occasional lunch too. They hadn't gone there for dinner often, but she knew they'd be open until nine. Just pulling into the small parking lot filled her with nostalgia.

She hadn't allowed herself to think about her life with Brock. The only way to survive in an undercover assignment like this was to immerse yourself into the role. As if she wasn't Brock's wife and fellow cop.

She was Feng Chi, a woman involved in Muchin's sex-trafficking operation. Of course, her girls were not given to prostitution rings the way Muchin paid her to do. She managed to help them escape but provided the cash to Muchin as if they were on the job.

Constantly walking a fine line between saving girls and being caught and killed.

But now she sat in her car, staring at the restaurant desperately wishing she could just walk back into Brock's arms, leaving the horrifying world of sex trafficking behind. Especially since she hadn't been able to find and rescue Mai Shi.

It was tempting to put the gear shift into reverse and drive far away from there. But she couldn't do that to Brock.

Not again. Leaving him the first time had been difficult

enough.

Drawing in a deep breath, she shut down the car and slid out from behind the wheel. She headed inside, easily spotting Brock in the corner booth.

Their booth.

His green gaze pierced hers as she moved forward. His expression remained hard as stone, without an ounce of welcome or compassion.

His frank hostility caught her off guard.

"I guess I should be honored you kept your word for once," he said as she slid across from him.

She shrugged. "I told you I would."

"You said a lot of things, Liana," he shot back. "Like 'until death do us part.'"

It was no surprise he'd tossed their wedding vows into her face. She'd known she'd hurt him, but she also wasn't going to sit here like a lamb, tolerating his verbal punching. She held his gaze. "Be civil or I'm gone."

Brock's gaze narrowed. He opened his mouth, then seemed to think better of it. A server came over with menus. "Can I get you anything to drink?"

"Coffee," she and Brock answered in unison.

The woman laughed. "I'll be right back."

There was a long silence before Brock spoke. "Who is Troy?"

She nodded, remembering their argument. She waited until their server brought their coffee before saying, "Troy Wallace. He's my handler in this undercover op."

"Are you sleeping with him?" Brock asked.

Her fingers itched to slap his face. "No, Brock. I'm working an undercover assignment. One I was forbidden to tell you about."

"That's insane. Why wouldn't you tell me about it?"

"Because you would have interfered. And don't try to pretend you wouldn't have."

He scowled but didn't argue. Her husband knew she was right.

"You saw my text messages because you went through my phone." She kept her voice even. "I assume you didn't trust me back then either, so it's no surprise you don't trust me now. That's your choice, Brock. I wouldn't have played up having a relationship with Troy if you hadn't jumped to that conclusion."

He scoffed. "You really expect me to believe that?"

"Not really." She shrugged, battling a sudden wave of exhaustion. "You're the only one who can decide what you believe. I can't force you or change your mind." She paused, then asked, "What happened to Bai Chow?"

"I asked my teammate Raelyn to book him on menacing with a deadly weapon." He played with a napkin, shredding it into small pieces. It was something Brock did when he was emotionally distraught. Not that he'd ever admit to such a thing. "Is Chow part of your undercover assignment?"

"Yes." She leaned forward. "What were you doing there, Brock? What made you come into the kitchen of Lu Chen in your uniform?"

He pushed the pile of shredded napkin aside. "I have no idea why I went inside. I ordered takeout and was going to use the bathroom. Hearing your low voices, I pushed the door to the kitchen open." He shook his head. "I was shocked to see you there."

She believed him, unlike the way he believed her. "Yeah, I was surprised to see you too. I can only hope you didn't completely blow my cover. I did my best to put the blame of your arrival on Bai Chow."

His gaze narrowed. "You're not seriously sticking with the assignment?"

When they'd first started dating, she'd been touched by the way he'd seemed so protective of her. Now it was downright annoying. "Yes, I am. So I need you to promise not to tell anyone about seeing me. Or what I'm doing." She frowned. "I hope you didn't tell Raelyn."

"I didn't, but I don't think it's smart of you to keep playing whatever role Troy has assigned. One hour ago, Bai was about to kill you."

"Because he thought I brought the police into the kitchen." She suddenly realized that agreeing to meet with Brock was a mistake. "Look, I came here as promised. Now it's your turn to uphold your end of the deal. Do not tell anyone within the tactical team about what I'm doing or go to Troy with this." She hesitated, then added, "Unless you hate me so much you want to see killed."

"Why are you doing this?" There was a hint of desperation in his voice. "There's no reason for you to put your life on the line."

For my mother. She didn't say the words, though, knowing he wouldn't understand. She rose to her feet. "I have to go. Thanks for the coffee."

"Liana, wait!"

She ignored him. Heading outside, the March wind kicked up, snatching the door from her fingers. Wrestling it closed, she turned to head toward her car. A nearby car was running. Then the window slowly rolled down.

Gun!

Liana hit the ground, rolling toward her sedan while pulling her weapon as gunfire shattered the silence of the night.

Made in the USA
Columbia, SC
16 January 2024

30554576R00134